Salt of the Earth

Kalindi Charan Panigrahi was a notable poet and writer in Odia. He is credited for the short but influential movement in Odia literature called the Sabuja Yug, which was the age of Romanticism, inspired by Rabindranath Tagore's writings. He was awarded the Padma Bhushan in 1971.

Leelawati Mohapatra published her first novel, *Hanging by a Tail*, in 2008 and after a long interlude is working on her next.

Paul St-Pierre is a former Professor of Translation Studies at Montreal University and has published several studies on translation theory and practice.

K.K. Mohapatra, an Odia writer, has published three collections of stories, a novel, two books of non-fiction, and an autobiography. He has also translated into Odia selected works of such writers as I.B. Singer, Jean-Paul Sartre, Franz Kafka, Gabriel Garcia Marquez, and William Shakespeare, to name just a few.

Together Leelawati Mohapatra, Paul St-Pierre and K.K. Mohapatra have translated extensively from Odia into English. Their books include, among others, *The HarperCollins Book of Oriya Short Stories* (1998), *Ants, Ghosts and Whispering Trees: An Anthology of Oriya Short Stories* (2003), *Fakir Mohan Senapati: The Brideprice and Other Stories* (2005), *The Greatest Odia Stories Ever Told* (2019), and more recently Fakir Mohan Senapati's iconic novel *Chha Mana Atha Guntha* (Six and a Third Acres).

KALINDI CHARAN PANIGRAHI

Salt of the Earth

Translated from the Odia by Leelawati Mohapatra,
Paul St-Pierre and K.K. Mohapatra

PENGUIN BOOKS
An imprint of Penguin Random House

PENGUIN BOOKS

USA | Canada | UK | Ireland | Australia
New Zealand | India | South Africa | China

Penguin Books is part of the Penguin Random House group of companies
whose addresses can be found at global.penguinrandomhouse.com

Published by Penguin Random House India Pvt. Ltd
4th Floor, Capital Tower 1, MG Road,
Gurugram 122 002, Haryana, India

First published in Odia as *Matira Manisha*, 1930
Published in English in Penguin Books by Penguin Random House India 2022

ISBN 9780143457961

Typeset in Bembo Std by Manipal Technologies Limited, Manipal
Printed at Replika Press Pvt. Ltd, India

www.penguin.co.in

Translators' Note

All families carry within their wombs the seeds of their own disintegration. There is an old Odia saying: *There will be as many homes as there are brothers*. Even a family of two sons eventually breaks up as the sons grow up and get married. Once married, so the belief goes, they fall under the spell of their scheming and wicked little wives. As another Odia proverb has it: *How can the nightly whisperings of a woman who shares a bed with a man ever fall on deaf ears*. As long as the parents are alive, the cracks are papered over. But after they are gone the final rift and partition of family property inevitably follow. The sheer quantity of novels, short stories, sociological studies and tomes that have been expended on this subject is mind-boggling.

So why on earth should a slim novel like *Matira Manisha* on this all-too-familiar, if not hackneyed, theme attract instant notice and success? And one written by a 'green' author[1] who had under his belt only a small body of poetry.

The answer, paradoxically, lies in the well-worn theme of the novel. Almost all readers had first-hand knowledge of family partitions; they knew the stages, the circumstances of family feuds. They read in the novel their own experience and recognized its commonplace characters: two daughters-in-law nurturing their own grievances; two sons, one breaking his back over raising crops and the other, a wastrel, gallivanting around the village; a vicious man stoking the embers of jealousy and anger.

The critics too were impressed and fulsome in their praise. Lila Ray, the novel's first translator, and her co-author Narendra Misra pointed out, the book was remarkable 'not only for its depiction of enduring human values but also for its realistic portrayal of the culture of rural Odisha'.[2] Madhusudan Pati, the author of a critical monograph on Panigrahi, said, '*Matira Manisha* marks an astonishing creative achievement—astonishing because, it has a plot that is disarmingly bare . . . with nothing particularly subtle or profound about its thematic design, and nothing very highly skilled or mature about its craftsmanship . . .'[3] Nearly every other critic, Subha Chakraborty Dasgupta among them, has underlined the novel's 'stark simplicity'.[4] Its appearance was at once a great literary, social and political event, according to Ganeswar Mishra.[5] A 'landmark creation . . . which constituted a significant distinction in the growth of Oriya novel since Phakirmohan', as viewed by Jatindra Mohan Mohanty.[6]

*

Defying all logic and expectation, not only did the novel get issued in a large print run of one thousand and a half—not even Fakir Mohan Senapati's iconic *Chha Mana Atha*

Guntha had had as large a print run on its debut—normally reserved only for the reprints of the scriptures and the puranas; but its popularity was immense.

The phenomenal critical and commercial success, way beyond Panigrahi's wildest dreams, unfolded itself in forty editions of the novel in the first thirty years—a literary feat that had eluded all his far more illustrious predecessors, including even the great master Fakir Mohan Senapati.

Matira Manisha has never been out of print since its debut in December 1930. A few carping detractors have attributed this to its selection as a textbook, ignoring the fact that there must be something fundamentally strong, wholesome and enduring in appeal in order for any novel to be selected as a textbook in the first instance, and secondly, the fact that the selection in the case of this particular novel held good only for a decade or so. But the book has remained in print long after it ceased being a college text. In its enduring appeal, as Sisir Kumar Das observed, *Matira Manisha* (1930) easily compared to something as deep and vital as Premchand's *Godan* (1936).[7]

Obviously, Panigrahi succeeded in making his novel resonate with the readers in some elemental way. He connected the action taking place in a small village (less than a speck of dust compared to the immensity of the cosmos, as he hurries to liken it to in the prefatory lines of the book) to something very significant taking place in a much bigger arena. What he did was to connect the conduct of the main protagonist with what Mahatma Gandhi was doing at the national level: unleashing the power of the weapon of passive resistance, which in turn had its inspiration in the Ramayana. All without mentioning Gandhi or the Ramayana even once in the novel.

*

Written presumably sometime in the summer of 1925, as evident from the reading of Panigrahi's autobiography *Ange Jaha Nibheichi* (1978) but published five years later in the winter of 1930,[8] *Matira Manisha*, literally 'the men of the soil', is considered as one of the early, if not the earliest, works of fiction in any Indian language to pay homage to Gandhian ideals and philosophy. '*Matira Manisha*,' as historian Biswamoy Pati observed, 'epitomises the interaction of Gandhian idealism with Oriya literature.'[9]

*

Kalindi Charan Panigrahi (1901–1991), who was twenty-four years of age when he wrote this debut novel, had already been through the heady influence of romantic idealism and revolutionary radicalism while still in Ravenshaw College, where he spent four years and from where he graduated in 1923. (Although the spirit of the Progressive Writers' Movement, which would grip many a young writer, including his own younger brother—Bhagabati Charan Panigrahi, who became a card-carrying member of the Communist Party of India, and who would be credited with putting Odisha on the geopolitical map of the Party—was still a few years away, socialism as a practising socio-political ideal had already gained considerable popularity among young and educated Indians following the success of the Russian Revolution in 1918.) While still an undergraduate, this starry-eyed young man with a hunger for words had played a leading role in bringing into being a literary band known as the 'Greens' with some like-minded friends, among them Annada Sankar Ray, Baikuntha Patnaik, Harihar Mahapatra and Sarat Chandra Mukherjee. Among them they published a copious amount of romantic poetry, much of which would be forgotten all too soon, and would be dismissed by critics like Mayadhar Mansinha as unsure of 'what it believed in or what it wanted to destroy'.[10]

But although the euphoric 'Green' period of Odia literature of the 1920s proved fragile and short-lived, and the group disintegrated inside of a decade, individually its members thrived and went on to establish firm reputations of their own as writers of substance. Of them all, Panigrahi established the most solid reputation, being the most prolific and versatile.

*

As alluded to in Panigrahi's autobiography *Ange Jaha Nibheichi* (1978), the idea of this rather simplistic social novel about rural folks practically fell into his lap when a migrant farmhand in Kujang—where, after college, the young author had started working in the cooperative department of the government of Odisha—narrated to him one evening

the true account of two brothers caught in the throes of
a family partition. The story left an indelible impression
on Panigrahi's mind. Panigrahi came from a joint family
himself. (He was between two brothers, both having literary
aspirations and achievements. His father, of a philosophical
bent of mind, had also been a writer.) This impression
was indelible not because this particular story of a family
squabble, a feud and partition had some surprising or unique
elements, or something totally out of the way, but because
the older of the feuding siblings had taken the unheard of
and unprecedented step of relinquishing his share and every
bit of the family property to his younger brother and had
walked out of home with his wife and children. It was
not every day, or every other day, that an incident of this
kind took place when one legitimate claimant to ancestral
property walked out not in a huff but cheerfully without
a trace of ill will or rancour. The story hit Panigrahi, who
came from a joint family having strong village roots although
his father had set up a successful legal practice in town, so
hard that he couldn't remain in peace until he had fashioned
a novel out of it within a couple of months.

*

When the time came to making his foray into fiction,
Panigrahi found nothing more inspiring than the path-
breaking social realism which Fakir Mohan Senapati (1843–
1918), the father of modern Odiya prose, had pioneered
with his iconic novel *Chha Mana Atha Guntha* (1897). Now,

additionally, under the spell of Gandhianism sweeping the land, Panigrahi wanted his fiction to not only present the mirror image of the society in which he lived but also to subtly change it in the direction desired by Gandhi. He had come to cherish, albeit wistfully, as did the vast majority of writers of his generation, that the pen was mightier than the sword, that literature could alter life. No wonder this maiden novel of his has often been viewed as an unabashed paean to Gandhian idealism, and his protagonist, Baraju Pradhan, as a 'mini-Gandhi'.[11] Yet, as much as he painted an idealized picture of the main protagonist, he did not try to glamourize the village and village life.

The language of the book is an embodiment of the purely rustic, the colloquial—'a language of clay and wattles' as Pati noted.[12] It has been described as 'colloquial and intimately rural' by Ganeswar Mishra.[13] K. Satchidanandan found in it 'the fragrance of popular speech'.[14] Critics like Subha Chakraborty Dasgupta noticed in his language an effort to 'not separate the narrator from the narratee'.[15]

The language of *Matira Manisha* is an unadorned, guileless, earthy argot favoured mainly by the rural, agrarian folks of Cuttack and Puri districts. (Panigrahi came from a village not far from Bhubaneswar and was educated in Puri and Cuttack towns.) The utter colloquial tone of the novel is all the more evident when his characters tend to philosophize. They find earthy equivalents of Sanskritized words and usages to express themselves. (It once again underlines the young author's strenuous effort to refrain from glamourizing.) No double entendres for him, no euphemisms, no cloaked expressions,

no linguistic acrobatics, no sly and subversive wit of the kind
Senapati (and his illustrious contemporary Gopal Chandra
Praharaj, the encyclopaedist) revelled in. He shunned the
maestro's copyrighted brand of biting humour and boisterous
playfulness of language. Truth to say, imitation would only
have worked to his detriment.

Nor did Panigrahi make an effort to match Senapati's
free-wheeling range of references to experiences and
events worldwide. He favoured to focus on the microcosm:
one peasant family; on just one crisis overtaking this
little family in the form of partition of parental property
between two brothers following the death of their
parents. Right from the first paragraph of the novel, he
made it crystal clear that he wasn't making it his business
to paint the big picture; on the contrary, he chose to stay
focused on the small. The bigger world is so tightly shut
out of the narrative that critics have wondered how the
novelist could manage to do just that in the India of the
1930s, when colonial rule was so much the way of Indian
life. There was never even a casual or stray reference to
the political climate or situation obtaining in the country.
Says Anuradha Goyal:

> One big observation I had from this book was there was
> no mention of British Raj, though in early 20th CE it
> was at its peak. There is no mention of any kings or
> administrators. It seems as if the village is a universe of
> its own, though there is a mention of going to Cuttack
> and Calcutta.[16]

By not trying to match Senapati, Panigrahi unwittingly ensured that his novel would have its own, and wider, appeal. Unlike the iconic *Chha Mana Atha Guntha*, it could be read and readily understood by anyone and everyone, as much by village folks as by town folks, readers of both sexes, of all ages; it didn't call for any high degree of awareness of the various levels of literary engagement with a text. No wonder, therefore, that while Senapati's masterpiece was, and continues to remain, a connoisseur's delight, *Matira Manisha* remains a firm favourite of the so-called literary hoi-polloi. Just about anybody who knows his alphabet can read and grasp it.

*

Much has been made of the open-endedness of the novel. The younger brother, full of remorse and repentance, goes looking for the elder brother. Not to beg him to return home, but to tag along with him wherever he is headed. The elder brother, amused, sends him packing with a gentle admonition, which, in Odia, goes like this: '*Chhi, chhi, maichia toka!*' This is the last sentence of the novel. Word for word it translates: *chhi* tut/ugh/come on/shame on you; *maichia* effeminate/sissy/spineless/weakling/someone tied to his wife's sari-end/apron strings; *toka* boy/young fella.

The choice of the last words of the novel is significant. The brotherly banter denotes that in spite of their differences, the elder retains some affection for the younger.

At a deeper level, the bond between them remains intact, and the novel ends on a note of hope. All unhappy families may break up and give rise to happy families, which then grow into unhappy families before they too come apart at the seams. This is a universal, inevitable cycle. Life goes on. Day follows night follows day . . .

At a time when the reading public was not exposed to the tradition of sequels, *Matira Manisha* strongly suggested a sequel. Would Baraju return home someday? What would become of his wife and children, how would they survive? Would Baraju make his way to the nearest town, or settle down in another village, to earn a living? Would Chhakadi, the younger brother, follow him into exile? What would become of his childless wife? Not until 1947, when *Luhaara Manisha* (Men of Iron) appeared, would the reader be any the wiser. (Incidentally, *Luhaara Manisha* bombed. As did the last in the trilogy, *Aajira Manisha* [Today's Men], which came out in 1957.) Never since Upendra Kishor Das's *Malaajanha* (Day Moon, 1928), a bitter-sweet story of illicit love, had a novel so tantalizingly left readers in a feverish state of anticipation.

Notes

1. The 'Sabuja' (literally, Green) phase of Odia literature, to which Kalindi Charan Panigrahi owed his debut as a writer, was a short-lived experiment between 1920 and 1930, roughly corresponding to the 'Chhayabadi' period of Hindi literature and 'Rabikiran' period of Maratha literature. The

'Green' writers were heavily influenced by the writings of Rabindranath Tagore.

2. Lila Ray and Narendra Misra, 'Kalindi Charan Panigrahi: Poet and Intellectual', *Indian Literature*, Vol. 11, No. 3, July–September 1968, p. 101. Lila Ray's translation *A House Undivided* was published in 1973. A second translation of the novel titled *Born of the Soil* (Niyogi, New Delhi, 2017) has been done by Bikram K. Das.

3. Madhusudan Pati, *Kalindi Charan Panigrahi*, Sahitya Akademi, New Delhi, 2001, p. 20.

4. Subha Chakraborty Dasgupta, 'Revisiting Kalindicharan Panigrahi: A Centenary Tribute', *Indian Literature*, Vol. 46, No. 5, September–October 2002, p. 139.

5. Ganeswar Mishra's short note on *Matira Manisha* in *Encyclopaedia of Indian Literature*, Vol. 3, Sahitya Akademi, New Delhi, 1987.

6. Jatindra Mohan Mohanty, *History of Oriya Literature*, Vidya, Bhubaneswar, 2006, pp. 365 and 405.

7. Sisir Kumar Das, *A History of Indian Literature 1911–1956*, Sahitya Akademi, New Delhi, 1995, Reprint 2006, p. 281.

8. Catalogue of Books and Periodicals published in the Province of Bihar and Orissa, and registered Under Act XXV of 1867, during the quarter ending the 31st March, 1931, p. 9. The year of publication has often erroneously been given as 1931 by some, 1933 by several others, even as 1934 by one.

9. Biswamoy Pati, *Situating Social History: Orissa, 1800–1997*, Orient Longman, 2001, p. 85.

10. Mayadhar Mansinha, *A History of Oriya Literature*, Sahitya Akademi, New Delhi, 1962, second printing, 2005, p. 234.

11. Das, *A History of Indian Literature 1911–1956*, p. 75.

12. Madhusudan Pati, *Kalindi Charan Panigrahi*, p. 22.

13. Ganeswar Mishra's short note on *Matira Manisha* in *Encyclopaedia of Indian Literature*, Vol. 3, Sahitya Akademi, New Delhi, 1987.

14. K. Satchidanandan, 'Kalindicharan Panigrahi: A Centenary Tribute', *Indian Literature*, Vol. 46, No. 5, September–October 2002, p. 133.

15. Dasgupta, 'Revisiting Kalindicharan Panigrahi: A Centenary Tribute', p. 141.

16. Anuradha Goyal, 'Born of the Soil by Kalindi Charan Panigrahi, Tr. Bikram K. Das', 28 February 2017, *anureviews.com*.

SALT OF THE EARTH

1

Millions of suns rise and set in the ordered universe, among them our very own, old familiar Sun. Around each revolve, spinning like tops, countless planets and satellites, among these our celestial body—Mother Earth. On its surface, a tiny country—India. Within this country, the state of Odisha; within Odisha, the district of Cuttack; and in this district, on the banks of the Birupa, Pradhan Colony, an ordinary settlement of ordinary people. In the middle of this colony, Shyam Pradhan's tiny mud hut. Compared to the vastness of the cosmos, what does it amount to—a speck, an atom—who can say? Days follow nights; seasons flow into each other; months and years pass.

Who first set foot on this tiny strip of land? Not a single footprint has been left behind. Who first cultivated these lands, sowing and reaping? Only the flowing Birupa would know, along with the sun and the moon, of course. But today the land around Pradhan Colony is radiant with golden rice paddy, alive with the joyous cacophony of human voices. Hundreds of children have played in its dust and passed on. Just as have seven and more generations of Shyam Pradhan's ancestors, and as did, Shyam Pradhan himself in his childhood. The riverbank has reverberated with the ululations of the village women celebrating festivals of all kinds. And it is here that funeral pyres have blazed too, the dry summer sands of the riverbed flooded with the tears of the widows and the bereaved come to take their ritual baths. Who can say how long all this has been going on?

History has no record of Shyam Pradhan's ancestor, who first settled here. The reigns of the Hindus, the Muslims, the Marathas have succeeded one another—kings have come and gone, dynasties risen and fallen. Tidal waves of religions have swept the earth—Hinduism, Buddhism, Islam and Christianity! But no visible signs of any of this can be found in Pradhan Colony. It is like the grass, humble and eternal— storms and high winds may uproot mighty trees, but the news of their devastation never reaches the grass below. The same holds true for Shyam Pradhan's mud hut—not even a stone step was ever added to it; no member of this family ever wasted a fortune on riotous revelry; not a single one ever amassed a fortune lending money or hoarding paddy.

Since time immemorial the faith and devotion of people here have centred on the smooth black marble image of Goddess Mangala at the foot of an ancient hibiscus tree. Mother Mangala for everything, for every occasion: to ward off outbreaks of cholera and smallpox; to celebrate weddings and full-moon festivals; to make barren trees produce; to heal ailing children; to counter inauspicious dreams; to celebrate the first bunch of bananas or the first ridge gourd—the goddess is given every scrap of news, good and bad, sad and happy. So thickly smeared with layers of vermilion and oil is her image that not even one inch of free space can be found.

This is Pradhan Colony for you—ancient, small, and as ordinary as they come.

Of all its houses, Shyam Pradhan's is the most well known, despite the lack of stone slabs for its steps and bricks for its walls.

God knows how many times in the past it collapsed into rubble. Mud walls and a straw roof couldn't be expected to brave rain and storm for long—no more than ten years at a pinch. But that was long enough. No worries for a whole decade! As long as the wheel of Time kept rolling on. Shyam Pradhan's father and uncles—he had seen what large, strapping, energetic men they were—built new houses on the ruins of the old in only a couple of days, wet clay slapped onto bamboo slats. Shyam Pradhan too did the same—all with his own hands. Three times his house fell into ruin during his lifetime, three times he built it anew.

*

The house of Shyam Pradhan became a landmark not because of its size or splendour but because of the sterling character of the head of the family, Shyam Pradhan himself. Beggars and mendicants wandering into the village in search of alms were always directed to his house. When disputes between villagers deepened and fights broke out, whether here or elsewhere, it was Shyam Pradhan who was called upon to resolve them. If anyone fell sick or was visited with some calamity, it was to Shyam Pradhan people turned. If someone wanted to draw up a list of wedding purchases, it was Shyam Pradhan who had to be consulted. But for all that, Shyam Pradhan's formal learning didn't extend beyond the ability to read just the Bhagavat. He was not well versed in law, medicine or accountancy. But still, people had great confidence in him. He wouldn't let anyone down, no matter the job—getting Nidhi, the country doctor, to attend to a sick person in the middle of the night, obtaining the bark of a medicinal plant or looking after the welcome and comfort of a visiting wedding party and their musicians! And there was nothing in it for him—he didn't make money. Would he stoop so low as to look for personal gain? Didn't God provide him with enough to live by!

If somebody in trouble did not ask him for help, he would seek them out: 'Why didn't you inform Shyam? Is he already dead? Things take place right next door and he doesn't get to hear of it right away—shame on Shyam!'

Sometimes bitterness between people would reach a boiling point—skulls would split, a host of litigations begin, families totter on the brink of ruination. It was Shyam Pradhan who would come forward to make peace. He would coax, cajole and beg—fondle a chin, grasp hands, even fall at someone's feet—and if none of that worked he'd go on a fast. 'Do all your fighting once poor old Shyam Pradhan's dead and gone, won't you. Slap court cases on one another, drag yourselves to the police station, whatever— but not as long as he's alive and kicking!'

'Why fight?' That was his argument. 'Life's so short! Generations of our ancestors have fought and disappeared—the soil they tilled has outlived them all. Has the land increased by even an inch? An acre remains an acre, no more, no less. We too will go, as will our children and, afterwards, our grandchildren and their grandchildren, and all this—the land, farmyards and houses—will be left behind. All that will remain of us will be tiny mounds of ashes on the sands of the Birupa, along with a few potshards and charred wood from the funeral pyres, until they too are washed away by the floods, leaving no trace of them behind.'

He was plain spoken, not a man who thinks one thing but says another. Even to the high and mighty, whether kings or princes, he would speak his mind, regardless of consequences. Yet the very next day he would volunteer to slave away for them, lending a hand to raise a beam of wood to rebuild a man's house; scouring, if necessary, more than half-a-dozen villages to bring medicine to a man's pregnant wife going into labour. No wonder he was looked up to, his word scripture. People valued his opinion over everyone else's put together.

*

The woman Shyam Pradhan had married was just as good. She might have come from lowlier stock, but narrowness of heart didn't define her. Even when she had barely enough for her own family, she wouldn't turn away a neighbour. She'd turn her pots and pans upside down, shake out whatever they contained and pack some food for her. 'So what if I'm left with nothing! If I come to your rescue today, tomorrow someone will come forward to help me out.'

Her housekeeping was the subject of local folklore. 'That Pradhan woman, she's truly unique! How she finds space in that tiny house of hers for every pot, pan, pail and vessel she owns! And mind you, none are empty; there's always a little something in every one them, rice, pulses, legumes, cereals or mustard seeds. And God knows what black magic she practises on that skinny old cow of hers— how does it yield so much? How does she manage to make curd, butter and ghee for her guests and visitors?'

'People like her,' Saradi Bou would comment, 'are from another time. Do you know she beats her daughters-in-law if they haven't left their beds before dawn? Sometimes they're still asleep by the time the old woman's through with sweeping the courtyard and swabbing it with cow-dung paste. She keeps the dirt floor so spick and span you could eat off it!'

'That's not all,' chipped in Sevati. 'Remember the bumper mango crop we had some years ago? The old woman still has reserves of pickles she made that year, you know. The tiniest bite and even a woman who's given birth and lost all her appetite will begin to crave food, and how!'

*

The old lady had had her two sons after a million prayers to gods and goddesses of all kinds, and after many fasts, vigils and

penances—Baraju and Chhakadi. But she never ventured to
call them by their names. If she were asked why not, she
would laugh: 'What's in a name, huh, and these insignificant
little tadpoles, why on earth should I call them by their
names? The older one she called 'Shashukhia', the death of
his mother-in-law, and the younger 'Master of Mischief'.

As much as she adored her boys, her two daughters-
in-law didn't meet with her approval. A woman's life,
in her view, counted for nothing, didn't matter, was the
lowliest and most miserable of all forms of life. She herself
had gone through hell when she had started out as a new
wife and daughter-in-law. She had received her fair share
of blows, bruises and scolding, which she had put up with
without demur; she had simply stuck it all out. A woman's
life was devoted solely to her husband and children—they
were the ruling passions of her life, her chief delights.
Food and clothing for her own self weren't essential. A
woman shouldn't look to herself—she mustn't look for any
comfort. Who could say how much sin it took for a soul
to be born and condemned to live as a woman? Sometimes
when the two daughters-in-law picked a fight and went
at each other, she would say, 'A woman's life is the worst;
only a wretched sinner is born as a woman. So what are
you two up to, why are you screaming and shouting, why
are you at each other's throats? All that can result in is
splitting up the family, isn't that right? But tell me why.
Why not take a leaf from the two brothers? Do you see
them fighting? Doesn't the family belong as much to them
as it does to you?'

Occasional reprimands and upbraiding were absolutely necessary: how else would the two young women learn to live together? One was from a place named Kantapada and the other from Narada. Since, unlike the two brothers, they had not been born of the same womb, how could they care, be bothered about and have feelings for each other?

But unlike other mothers-in-law, the old lady never subjected her daughters-in-law to physical torture or ill-treatment. After all, they were outsiders; if she didn't look after them in the beginning, who would? But they were not as dear to her as Baraju and Chhakadi, not in the same league. Sons, as the saying goes, come ahead even of gods! This was why the old lady would blow her top if she found nobody around to serve Baraju food before he set out for the fields in the morning, or if Chhakadi had to search for a little oil for his body before he had a bath. 'What are you two cows here for?' she would scream at her two daughters-in-law. 'To strut about like society ladies, your noses in the air?'

Of the two, she had a soft spot for the younger—for no other reason than that she was young, raw and callow. That's the way the world works—people are kinder to the young and helpless. She routinely and unfailingly inquired after the welfare of Chhakadi's wife: had she taken her bath, had she eaten, had she combed and braided her hair, was she regularly applying turmeric paste to her skin?

The older daughter-in-law resented the attention lavished on the younger. She was so swollen with pride as the mother of four children that her feet didn't touch the ground, and she wanted her parents-in-law, her husband—everyone—to

fuss and fawn over her. So whenever the mother-in-law said
to the younger woman, 'Come here, sit down so I can run a
comb through your tangled hair, which hasn't seen a drop of
oil in the last three days,' the elder would fume. 'Woe is me,
is she a little girl needing to be fussed over?'

The old mother-in-law would laugh at her. 'Ask
yourself, you peasant woman, didn't I fuss over you like
that when you first stepped into my home?'

'Oh, who bothers to fuss over a girl from a poor family!'
the elder daughter-in-law would mutter under her breath
in annoyance.

'What a liar you are! But have you ever looked after this
slip of a girl, have you ever inquired whether she's eaten?
Ever offered to comb her hair even if you saw it was tangled
and untidy? On top of all that, you're always ready to take
things personally!'

Like a cobra raising its hood when its tail is trodden on,
the elder daughter-in-law would rear up. 'What, a mere slip
of a girl, is she? Younger than my Hira and Suna, huh? My,
has she even been weaned? When my little kids are dying
of hunger, does anyone come forward to cook them a little
rice porridge or offer them a bowl of watered rice? Why
should I kill myself to serve like a slave in this house?'

'Hey, you can't possibly be so jealous of the younger
one! It's your job to mould her. She'll turn into what you
want only if you teach her.'

'Oh yes, some people are only waiting for *me* to teach
them! Why don't *you* teach her? As if she's dying to carry
out every wish of yours!'

That would rile the old woman up. 'What's the point in teaching *her*? What good did all that teaching do for you? You're both free to do as you please. As long as I have a patch of leafy greens in my backyard and a drumstick tree, I don't want either of you to do anything for me.'

For the old lady the patch was like a book of scripture, to be wrestled with, morning and evening. Whenever you looked for her you'd find her in the backyard harvesting the greens with a blunt sickle. Her chores seemed confined to amusing her grandchildren with bedtime stories, pruning the plants and occasionally bossing over her daughters-in-law.

Over time, a large part of the housekeeping had passed into the hands of the elder daughter-in-law. She looked after what was most important—income and expenses, who came in and who went out. She had also taken to bossing her younger sister-in-law, who had no choice but to put up with it.

People always think cattle or other dumb animals or deaf-mutes who can't speak don't feel anything and will put up with everything, with any beating and scolding. For the younger daughter-in-law it was no different; she had to endure it all. Only sometimes would the old mother-in-law take her side. But then she was an old, old woman and couldn't be expected to notice everything, and it made her very sad that someday, after she and her husband were gone, the family would split in two because of the daughters-in-law.

2

'The paddy's been out in the sun since this morning,' the elder daughter-in-law remarked acidly. 'Doesn't anyone think it should be turned over from time to time? Is no one else in the house doing any work because they don't have hands or legs? Is it up to me to do all the chores? Am I the only person who gets to eat?'

The old mother-in-law heaved a sigh when she heard this. 'Do you always have to try to make things worse? Aren't there any less poisonous words in your head? Do you wish to totally destroy this family?'

'Is that what you think, huh, Mother?' the elder daughter-in-law shot back. 'Just shows how much you understand, really! So, as far as you're concerned, it's up to me to put the paddy in the sun to dry, my job to pound it and remove the husk and then cook it too. Do all that and split this family in half as well! All the blame's on me, is it? The rest of the people in this house are saints, pure as holy tulsi, are they?'

The barb was aimed at none other than the younger daughter-in-law. She was the only daughter of a revenue supervisor and had been spoilt rotten. The dowry she brought at the time of her marriage left the neighbours cross-eyed with envy. It had made all the daughters in the village upset with their parents and turned the daughters-in-law green with shame and envy. Mothers-in-law cited her example whenever they scolded their daughters-in-law. 'Oh, you beggar's daughter,' they would scream whenever they had a chance. 'Don't get any notions! Have you stepped into my house covered in gold jewellery from head to toe, with ornaments on your ankles, wrists, nostrils and ears like the new daughter-in-law of the Pradhans?'

The younger daughter-in-law kept a low profile, shying away from everyone and not volunteering to do a spot of work around the house. For every little thing she had to be asked. After all, she was new to the family and, in the presence of her parents-in-law, couldn't come out in the open, let alone speak with anyone.

The old mother-in-law hadn't intended to irritate the elder daughter-in-law; it was never easy to win a war of words with her. Besides, truth to tell, it was she, the elder daughter-in-law, who did all the household chores. Since her arrival, the younger one had done nothing but sit like a stump, wallowing in her newness. She hadn't offered to take on even the smallest job, to break even a wisp of straw in half.

'Neti,' the old woman called out. 'Come here, girl, and turn the paddy grains over. I'm busy rubbing turmeric paste on Hara.'

'Good grief,' the elder daughter-in-law smirked. 'What honey in your voice! Someone's absolutely dripping with love and affection! Is that the best you can bring to your voice, Mother? Can't you do any better, any softer?'

With a long face, the younger daughter-in-law Neti, short for Netramani, went and turned the paddy over with her feet. What could she say in the presence of the mother-in-law? But as soon as the old woman was off to the backyard after rubbing turmeric paste on her granddaughter's skin, she began to mutter bitterly, 'Damn it, why am I being made the butt of rude remarks? What harm have I done anyone? Did I steal someone's bowl of food? Why is everyone in this family out to lord it over me with a spatula in hand?'

The elder daughter-in-law hurried off to the backyard to fetch their mother-in-law. 'You are always full of compliments for your younger daughter-in-law, thinking she would never say boo to a goose. Come and listen to how she's going on!'

When the old woman came back, she scolded her younger daughter-in-law. 'Shut up, girl. How dare you talk back to your elder sister! You aren't meant to!'

The younger woman clammed up. She couldn't attack her mother-in-law. After all, she was at her in-laws' place, not her father's, and the neighbours might criticize her as someone who hadn't been there even a year but was already beginning to show her true colours!

She kept her mouth shut until her husband came home. Then she gave him a blow–by-blow account, embroidering a bit as she went along. The spark she lighted that day would one day burst into flames. How long could the embers stay buried under the ashes?

*

Chhakadi was good for nothing, if ever anyone was, spending his time roaming around the village, sporting a colourful towel on his shoulder, rings in his ears and a gold toothpick between his lips. He carried a silver betel box under his arm, wore a black jacket over his white shirt and hung out with a gang of Calcutta-returned friends, frequenting fairs, festivals and carnivals. He came home only for his meals and, if they were even a moment late, he would break the clay pots and pans. His father dismissed all this as the tantrums of a naughty boy yet to be 'broken'; he would behave once responsibilities fell on him. His mother—the moment she heard his voice from the street—would alert her two daughters-in-law: 'Hey, girls, the brat's back. Get him food as quickly as you can. If he has to wait even the slightest he'll bring the house down!'

On the day of the big fair at Sunajodi, Chhakadi returned home at midnight, after having a grand old time gambling, riding the whirligig and watching the Ramleela performance. The children were used to going to bed at sundown, but were still awake and on pins and needles, waiting to see what their uncle would bring them from the fair. Only the youngest was fast asleep. But before falling asleep, he had made his sisters and grandma promise to wake him the moment his uncle arrived.

Shyam Pradhan and Baraju had long gone to bed after eating, but the old mother was still waiting to have her dinner with her son. Naturally, the two daughters-in-law were also waiting; they couldn't eat before their mother-in-law did, even if they were famished. The two elder granddaughters, Suna and Hara, were listening to the story their grandma was recounting:

'A small pond, a little pond
the waters of the small pond . . .
There were six brothers and they all had wives
but my husband was the prince among them all . . .'

'Mother!' Chhakadi's shouts could be heard from the road. 'Mother!'

The old woman hurried to the door. Thank God, the brat was back.

The two children followed behind to see what their uncle had brought from the fair. The younger of the two was told to go and wake the youngest so he wouldn't miss out.

Chhakadi had a basket-load of goodies: sweet coconut balls, puffed rice, betel leaves and areca nuts, potatoes and onions, as well as some other items.

The old woman tried to quieten the kids with handfuls of sweet coconut balls, but that wasn't enough. Wide-eyed, they waited for more. The youngest, rubbing sleep out of his eyes, came and nestled against his uncle.

'You've had sweets, children,' Chhakadi said, 'what else are you waiting for? Off to bed now.'

But that didn't stop the kids. They knew their uncle had brought toys for them but didn't want to beg.

Then Chhakadi fished a little red object from his pocket. Three pairs of eyes followed every movement of his hands.

A dramatic pause later, Chhakadi held it up to the lamp light: a small toy. What was it—a duck? It quacked when pressed.

'Now, who wants this?' Chhakadi asked.

Hands shot up, voices answered in chorus: 'I do! Give it to me. Uncle, give it to me.'

The duck went to the youngest.

Then from out of the uncle's bundle popped one by one—a rattle drum, a harmonica, a trumpet . . .

The kids started bickering over who would take what and there was a mighty din. Then one started blowing the trumpet. The racket went through the roof.

Old Shyam Pradhan woke up. 'That layabout hasn't been back more than a minute,' he swore at Chhakadi, 'but listen to the racket he's making! Get lost, you good-for-nothing! Cross the Black Waters or go to Calcutta or wherever and try make some money so you can look after us. Fat chance you'll ever do that. Will you ever leave the comforts of home?'

Seduced by the hairstyle of the Calcutta-returned young men in the village and their shiny metal briefcases, Chhakadi had often asked his father for permission to leave home and try his luck in Calcutta or beyond. But his father had always shot him down. 'Why, son, has the soil of your own village started to stink? There's a saying—the poor father hasn't a drop of oil for his hair while the son has enough for his seven-strand plait. Listen here, boy, seven generations of your ancestors stuck it out in this village and were none the worse for it. So why do you want to go elsewhere—to earn more money? You aim to build a palace or what?' Every time the old man wanted to berate Chhakadi for his faults, he came up with the same words.

Dinner over, Chhakadi headed for his bedroom—a tiny room, half the space taken by four straw-lined sacks of pulses, no cot. The bed on the mud floor was just a reed mat, over which lay a threadbare quilt stitched out of old and discarded clothes. On a tiny shelf dug into the wall stood a lamp lit by a wick soaked in *punnag* oil. The base of the shelf had turned black from the seeping oil, while the wall above it was pitch black with soot. From the bamboo rafters of the ceiling were suspended two bunches of paddy grain; tiny insects hovered around them. Beside these hung two more slings, each holding a clay bowl in which the old lady of the house stored mango pickles and mustard seeds. In a corner, two wicker boxes, one big and the other smaller, sat on a flat piece of mango wood. The larger was covered in big white patches, from people wiping their fingers on it after applying lime to their betel leaves.

Spiderwebs hung in every nook and corner. Two small house bats flitted in and out, gobbling up mosquitoes and insects. Beneath the sacks mice were busy, burrowing through the floor to get at the grain. In short, a cramped space crawling with insects and animals, which, out of pity, left a little room for humans to carry on with their lives.

But Chhakadi's room was no worse than the others in the house; if anything, the bedrooms of Shyam and Baraju were even more jam-packed. At least Chhakadi's bedroom wall was hung with pictures of Radha and Krishna; Shyam and Baraju's rooms were littered with bat droppings and heaps of loose soil dug up by mice. No matter how well the floors were swept and cleaned, the squalor returned the next day.

So that was all the space poor Chhakadi and his wife had to make do with. What choice did he have? He didn't have the resources to add a bigger room for himself. He had no say in the income and expenditures of the household; those were matters in the hands of his father and elder brother. He couldn't even afford to buy a new lantern and a good briefcase. His father had rejected all his pleadings to leave the village to seek his fortune. 'You don't have to leave your home only to serve under somebody else!' was the line the old man had consistently taken. Nor did his elder brother ever intercede on his behalf. So, although he didn't broadcast it, Chhakadi was sometimes very angry with them both.

Chores for the day done, Chhakadi's wife, Netramani, bustled into their bedroom, jangling her anklets. Without even a sideways glance at her husband, she spread the end of her sari on the floor by the door and lay down.

Chhakadi caught on. There must have been a fight.

'What's the matter?' he asked, smiling.

His wife didn't reward him with an answer.

He got up and tried to grasp her hands to raise her from the floor, but she pulled them away. 'Go shower all that love and concern on your elder brother, his wife and their children.'

'Hey, why are you so worked up? Let's talk.'

'What's there to talk about? Isn't there anyone else in this house to put paddy out in the sun and turn it over from time to time? Does no one else have legs and feet to do that? Would they get scalded and singed if they did? Damn it, I owe nothing to any hag or bitch! Why do I have to put up with their constant carping?'

'Why don't you give back as good as you get? Throw their words back at them!'

'How could I? Then the whole pack would be at my throat. If you can't stick up for me, why did you tie the knot with me?'

Slicing a betel nut with a sharp Achhutpur cutter, Chhakadi lowered his voice, 'What are you talking about? Elder sister-in-law can't order you around and get away with it. This home is not just hers, it belongs to you too. Who the hell is she to lord over you?'

His wife made a face. 'My, how well you make sense of what I'm trying to tell you! All I'm trying to say is she never tells me directly to do anything. Every order's indirect, roundabout and a sharp barb aimed at you know who.'

'Pay her back in her own coin, I say. Retaliate. Leave the consequences to me, I'll take care of them.'

'Oh really? Will you? As if you've taken care of everything until now. How many times have I told you to keep away from her children, not to spoil them with

affection and attention? I think I have a pretty clear idea
how deep your understanding goes, my husband!'

'Hey, listen. Don't misunderstand me. My old man
slipped me a few coins to buy toys and sweets for the
kids at the fair. Did you think I was spending from my
own pocket?'

'Wasn't there anyone else from the village going to
the fair?'

'If someone from the family was headed there, why
would the old man ask an outsider? Entrust precious money
to strangers, huh?'

Chhakadi had absolutely no problem reeling off one
lie after another, knowing only lies can placate women.
Netramani was welcome to look upon his elder brother
and his wife as her mortal enemies, but why drag the
blameless little children into the picture? What crimes had
they committed? He could never think of them as outsiders,
let alone enemies, no matter how bitter he might be. He
would always have a soft spot for them. In fact, he loved
them, kissed and fussed over them, hoisted them up on his
hips and shoulders, gave them sweets and toys. He would
still do all that, but only behind his wife's back from now
on. And he would warn the kids not to breathe a word of it
to their aunt: 'Carry tales to her, and the goodies will stop
forever, remember!'

3

Life . . . death, sleep . . . consciousness. Scattered with dreams. Separate states flowing seamlessly into each other. No conflict. Peaceful coexistence. Two sides of the same coin. Humans believe they control life, shape and influence it. Why then do they feel so helpless and full of despair in the face of death? They know everyone will die, leaving children and spouses behind. All are recalled from Earth. That's the law of Creation. Nobody can change that, nobody. Fleeting is human life.

The moment of recall had struck Shyam Pradhan's homestead. First it was the old woman's turn, and fair enough too. The old will be replaced by the young; white hair will change again to black. The old should never linger.

The two daughters-in-law massaged the old lady's feet. The grandchildren ran their tiny hands over her forehead. Chhakadi sat beside her, reading the holy Bhagavat aloud. The room, lit by a dim lamp, lay half in darkness. The faint light symbolized the fading of human life—the oil that had kept it burning until now had run low.

The flame sputtered, casting long shadows across the walls. The old woman had nothing else to experience; her days were done. It was time to take leave of the grandchildren, sons and daughters-in-law, husband, home and hearth. She was finished with all that—the patch of greens, the backyard, the homestead and more. She would leave all of that behind.

The news of her passing took no time to reach the homes in Pradhan Colony and beyond.

That woman was a noble soul, people commented, to have the good fortune of dying at a ripe old age, with vermilion shining in the part in her hair, with her husband outliving her, and on the auspicious day of an *ekadasi* too!

No one saw Shyam Pradhan cry as he led the funeral procession, throwing coins and grains of rice along the path. 'I won't have to carry on alone for long,' he said. 'Six months, or a year at a pinch. Surely my old woman can do without me in the foreign land that little while!'

The world continued as before. Nothing changed because Shyam Pradhan's old woman was gone—not one bit, not even by anything as slender as a thread. Our familiar Earth continued to turn around our familiar Sun, at its usual speed. In the Birupa, the water continued to flow as before, without a pause. Nothing came to a standstill for even a split second. The land, the harvest, incomes and expenses, the trees and the orchards—everything remained the same as before.

One day, old Shyam Pradhan called his elder son Baraju to his bedside. 'Son, I don't think I have much time left.

And you're rarely home because of your work. I'm afraid I might not get a glimpse of you when it's my time to pass. Who knows when that will be!'

Baraju was not highly educated or anything; he had only finished the village grammar school. But even with such a meagre education he could easily have become a zamindar's accountant or a lawyer's assistant, or at least a land surveyor. In fact, for two short spells he had been a zamindar's accountant before becoming a land surveyor. But his father had nagged him to quit. 'Why do you have to do a job, son? We're small people; with our humble needs, we don't require a lot of money to get by. We don't have to put on airs. Seven generations of our ancestors have made do with tilling the soil, and so shall we. Do we hope to get to heaven by exchanging our ploughshare for a pen?'

Baraju had come round to his father's point of view. Being in someone's employment and toadying to him while lording it over others was no good in the end. Bossing people around was as demeaning as being bossed around. But he had a family to support, hungry mouths to feed, hungry bellies to fill. So, although his father had often told him to quit his job, he had always parried with, 'All right, I'll quit. Just give me some time.' Besides, no job was permanent; jobs were as fleeting as the shadow cast by a slender palm tree, gone in moments. Why should he be a slave to them? Sometimes he would argue with his old man. 'Quitting is easy. I can quit any time. But we need to decide that only after due deliberation. If I quit my job, we might not be able to buy the little chunks of land we've been adding to our holding every year.'

The old Pradhan had smiled at Baraju's naivety. 'Son, trying to save money is madness. Why save if your children shape up well? And again, why save if they end up squandering everything? Saving is never an ideal.'

'Are you arguing it's a sin to save?'

'Not just an ordinary sin, but one of the deadliest. It's nothing but stealing, similar to daylight robbery. Think of someone like Hari Mishra in this village. How many helpless people, widows and waifs among them, has he ruined trying to get richer? Is that really wealth? More like the fiery breath of those he has exploited! And one day, that very breath will reduce Mishra to cinders—everything he has accumulated will go up in smoke, turn to ashes. All that you're making out of sorting the land records—that's poison too. That money will bring you no good.'

But Baraju had never asked for more than his legitimate fee, which surprised most people. 'Why, that's like taking the Lord's name in the land of the Devil! It wouldn't be more appropriate to take Rama's name in the land of Ravana! What's the point of being a settlement surveyor if you don't make money on the side? We've been through not just one, but two settlements, but this kind of honesty is unheard of. Our mortal eyes haven't seen another like Baraju, neither have our ears heard of one.'

Truth to tell, Baraju was honest to the bone, without a shred of greed. He never demanded even an aubergine from his clients, let alone money.

'Son,' the old man went on. 'I know about you; you do your job only for the salary you're paid; you don't touch an illegitimate coin. But tell me, who pays your salary? Did your father set up a fund for it? No matter what you say, your salary's also stolen money. Every official's a thief. Whose money is your salary paid from? The money of the poor. Who pays for the bosses and all their bossing, perks and privileges? Those who have to make do with only one meal out of four a day. Who made all these factories, mills, railways and ships, buildings possible? The poor. With their blood, to the last drop. Did you think a few officers and officials made all this possible?' The old man's eyes teared up, his chest heaved; he seemed to be chastising him on behalf of the wretched of the earth.

Baraju's blood boiled. 'You mean every official, policeman, lawyer, rich person and zamindar is immoral?'

'I didn't say they all are. They do save us from thieves, thugs, pickpockets and cut-throats. If someone commits a crime, he receives just punishment. If someone with more muscle power takes over someone else's land, he's hauled up in the law court. But all these criminals and thieves and thugs—where do they come from? They're a part of us, they come from us. Because we're rotten, we become criminals, and then we create judges, lawyers, officers and enforcers of the law. So what I always say is that the existence of the officials is nothing but the end result of our own wrongdoing—they're the products of our evil karma. The more crimes we commit, the bigger the tribe of lawyers grows. Would we need any of them if we always acted as we should? Why are there so many prisons, pounds and pens? Would there be any need for so many red-turbaned policemen?'

Baraju wouldn't give up. 'How do you accumulate merit and virtue? According to you, we shouldn't rise above our circumstances. We must stick to our station in life. The rich should continue to yoke us to ploughshares and push us with prods!'

'Son, whatever else you might be able to do with all your money, you can't buy merit and virtue. No amount of money will get you a ticket to heaven. You accumulate merit through your deeds—noble, selfless deeds worthy of a human being. Wherever, whenever you find crime and inequity rising, there you'll find human values taking a beating.' The old man smiled kindly. 'You have to relearn it all from the lowliest of the low—the cattle, sheep and goats, cats and dogs, ants, flies, mosquitoes.'

The old man's words rang very true. In his years of service, Baraju had seen how servility and the conditions of service had slowly sucked the goodness, kindness and sense of justice out of good human beings—how quickly simple and honest men had turned into bribe-taking monsters. Like Rahu, the evil planet, looming large over the moon during an eclipse. A poor, hard-working day labourer—how much did he earn? But he was the one who toiled to provide the world with food and clothing. What did he himself get to live on? Air? The world moved because of the labour of the poor, because they worked themselves to death. Did anyone acknowledge that at all?

Baraju decided to quit. He had had enough. Tilling the soil to make a living was what suited him best—seven generations of his ancestors had done just that. There was no shame in it.

Just as he had predicted, the old man got his summons inside of a year of his wife's passing. Welcoming it with a calm smile, he called Baraju to his deathbed. 'Son, my time's up. Look after yourselves. From now on you'll be responsible for the affairs of this family. I have only one wish. Guard against a family partition. Don't ever split up, you and your younger brother.'

The children, tutored and egged on by their mother, crowded around the old man. 'Grandpa, have you set aside a little nest egg for us? Have you hidden something of value somewhere in the house?'

The old man's eyes fluttered open, but he seemed to be looking for someone before closing them again.

The eldest granddaughter shouted into the old man's ear, 'Grandpa, do you have something hidden for us?'

The old man opened his eyes. The words seemed to reach him from a vast distance.

Chhakadi, who was sitting massaging his father's forehead, explained it to the dying man. Quite often doting old men and women salted away a little something for their grandchildren, to be handed over at the time of their death. Perhaps the old Pradhan was no exception.

The old man gave a wan smile, raising a finger upwards, towards heaven. 'Yes, I'm leaving a lot behind for you all: Dharma, merit. Follow Dharma forever.'

Then his eyes closed one last time.

His sons, daughters-in-law burst out bawling.

Some time later, wiping his eyes, Baraju began to make arrangements for the cremation. 'That's how things are,' he sighed. 'Life. Death. We must continue on.'

The news of Shyam Pradhan's passing spread in no time, and every family in the village felt bereaved, as if robbed of the head of their own family. What a sterling man he was, they all lamented. One in a thousand. All mortals came with only seven hands of land at birth, and that's all the land they would need for their funeral pyre when they passed; nobody was born immortal, imperishable or with a crown on their head, a head that would not know death. But sometimes the earth produced nuggets of gold. The old Pradhan was one of these. A man's worth, the saying goes, is appreciated only after he has passed. What matters is how people think and speak of him when he's gone.

The villagers all knew Baraju was ramrod straight and would keep true to his father. If his father rode a horse, he would ride an even more magnificent animal.

Baraju had taken after his father physically too. He was tall, broad, strong of limb. A turban wrapped around his head, he single-handedly looked after the cultivation of the family land, orchards and vegetable patches. Toiling from morning until night, he was constant in the care he took of the family, without a thought for his personal comfort. The only little thing he enjoyed was a mustard-oil massage of the soles of his feet before going to bed. Not for nothing his father had often repeated to him: 'A turban on his head and an oil massage of the soles of his feet—a man who regularly has both can hope to steer clear of doctors all his life!'

Baraju was indeed someone who never took ill, not even a headache to complain of. Summer or winter, rain or shine—he worked on his land through the four seasons. Even two people together could not heft the paddy bundles he made. When he started lifting water to irrigate his land, he would continue to work until after all the others had given up out of sheer exhaustion. The man was rock solid.

But what people respected him most for was his unshakable honesty. If he found a mound of gold on his path, he wouldn't give it even a second glance. If he owed anyone money, even for a coin that proved counterfeit, he made sure he paid it back double quick. Nobody had lost a paisa to him. No wonder the villagers all said it was safer to lend money to Baraju than place it in a vault. There might be departures in the rituals for Lord Jagannath, but no lapses were ever found in Baraju's commitments. He kept his word, no matter what, even if it seemed that might lead to his death and extinction.

His wife, however, was not cut from the same cloth. She was quarrelsome and picked fights at the flimsiest provocation. She was proud because she had given birth to not one but four children. Her feet never touched the ground—she demanded everyone's fawning attention. No wonder she and Baraju often locked horns. She just couldn't get along with her husband.

But Baraju had no time for cajoling, coaxing and bringing her around, for showering her with love and affection. During the day he didn't have a moment of respite and couldn't see what was taking place on the home front. Come evening, all he longed to do was gulp down his dinner and hit the bed.

His wife, her chores done, would often resort to the trick of massaging his feet to wake him up so she could give him the low-down on the doings of his younger brother and his wife. 'Things were under control as long as the parents-in-law were around. Now that they're gone, even nobodies have started flexing their muscles. That monkey of a man—your younger brother—has started calling me names. Just who does he think he is? How dare he insult me? A jackal daring to act the bully in a tiger's den? He doesn't exert himself to do an honest day's job, although he's able-bodied, all hale and hearty. He doesn't even bother to shoo off the cattle that stray into our ripening fields! He wouldn't care a bit if everything about this house went to rack and ruin. Does only one brother have to do every bit of work? Has anyone noticed how thin and gaunt he's become? All Chhakadi does is go roaming around the village, flitting from place to place, coming home only for his meals. On top of all that he calls me names. And that woman, his wife, refuses to break even a piece of straw in two; she doesn't seem to bother about where the next meal's coming from. But when it comes to fighting, the duo are like tigers and perfectly matched. If the husband calls someone a "bitch", the wife adds "barren" to it. Goodness, am I a beggar woman in this house? Have I been so utterly deserted? Don't I have anyone to defend my honour?'

But her husband was deaf to her words, having long fallen asleep. His snoring brought her acute disappointment.

What did it matter if the Lord Mahadev of a husband didn't listen to Hara Bou's nightly recitation of the scriptures? His younger brother's wife did. Ear pressed to the thin mud wall, Netramani eavesdropped on every word the elder sister-in-law spoke and relayed them to her husband when he returned home. 'You who sing your elder brother's wife's praises no end should hear all she tells her man. Do you imagine you're closer to your brother than his own wife? And that horrible woman, she weaves in so much, adds so much spice, tells so many lies. Naturally her husband starts fuming and fulminating against me: "Why is that woman simply filling her belly without doing a hand's turn? Does she imagine she can get her meals without doing a decent part of the household chores?" As if he's the one who's giving me my daily meals for free, hah! Who does all the cooking and serving and threshes the paddy in this household? I tell you, I'm done here, I can't take all the carping that goes on in this house. Let that bitch get into the act and cook and feed her brood from now on.'

Poor Chhakadi did not have the brains to make out that his wife's ravings and rantings were all vile lies. On the contrary, doubts began to assail him: Perhaps my elder brother isn't really who he seems to be? Is Hari Mishra's opinion of him on the mark? Is Baraju just a smooth-talker?

The village council president, Hari Mishra, couldn't stand it when people went overboard in their praise and

admiration for Baraju. He never missed a chance to find
fault with him. So Chhakadi had the rotten luck of having
to listen to his brother being reviled both inside and out
of the home. He couldn't stop the calumnies. Nor could
he open his mouth in front of his brother. His brother was
years older than him, by a decade or more. Even their home
was referred to as Baraju's rather than his; no one referred to
it as Chhakadi's house, even by mistake. After their parents'
death, he felt he had become more vulnerable. At home, his
wife was ever ready to stoke his anxiety.

*

Days passed. One day when he returned home from playing
cards, there was no milk in the pails and only one last handful
of rice sticking to the bottom of the pot. But his wife seemed
to take this worse than he did. 'Why on earth have things
come to this?' she complained to him. 'Have I got six or
nine husbands? I have only one, yet even he doesn't get to
eat his fill in this house! Why should I live here? Of what
use am I to him? I tell you, you should stick with your
brother, his wife and their children. I would be better off
at my parents', where I wouldn't have to go hungry, where
half a dozen outsiders get free meals every day.'

Words like these, which irritated Chhakadi in the
beginning, had gradually lost their sting—he had got
used to them. But how long could he live like a person
of no importance or authority? Natha Khatei and Halu
Sahu had separated from their brothers, but neither were

any the worse for it. On the contrary, they were better off than before. Both had opened shops and were making good money. What had he, Chhakadi, gained from not splitting from his brother? But how would he initiate the process of family partition? How would he bring up the topic?

4

Vast expanses of paddy fields stretching as far as the eye could see—and all so green. The Ashwina sky overhead so endless, so blue. The sun hot enough to melt a man's skull. Once in a while a wisp of cloud flirting with the sun and casting a pale shadow over the paddy fields below. Far off, the villages, tucked under the dense clusters of trees, nearly invisible. A gentle breeze, rising and falling, making its bashful journey over the green tops of the crop. Whoever was on high must have been struck dumb by the doings of mortals on Earth.

In some places, amidst all that beauty, were little broken men bent over at work in the fields. Elsewhere a cloud of egrets or green parakeets rose off one verdant patch to fly to the next, sometimes to the villages beyond. But the little brown men hunched over the paddy seedlings took no notice of anything around them. They were commonplace fixtures of the landscape—features of the fields, like the birds or the sun and the moon and the sky—unchanging, living the same way every one of the three hundred sixty-five days or twelve months or four seasons that made up a year, come rain or shine, chill or mist. Ages had already passed this way. People had remained the same; many hadn't been able to buy a long cloth to cover themselves from head to foot, nor an eight-hand towel in place of the narrower six-hand ones, so they could dress a bit more modestly. They had remained primitive men rather than become modern human beings. Clay. Soil. Mud. That's what they were—they worked with mud, soil, clay from birth to death. They were born of the soil, lived on it, lived off it; they built their homes on it and out of it; they dug it and grew paddy on it to keep their body and soul together. Earth people, earthlings, mud men, salt of the earth . . .

Among this toiling throng was Baraju Pradhan. A dirty towel around his waist and another wound around his head, he was hunched over paddy plants. God knows how many aeons had come and gone and how many generations of Barajus, enduring the sun on their bare backs, churning the mud underfoot, growing food; they had no hope, no fancy or florid language. They were blind even though they had eyes, deaf despite having ears, dumb even though having tongues—the deaf-mute-blind of the earth. They did not even take the full measure of their own suffering; they did not plead their own cause. They were like cattle, prodded, justly or unjustly, with a goad. They did not complain if they did not get their four meals a day.

Jadu Dalei, a neighbour and distant cousin, was working on his patch of land and exchanging idle chatter with Baraju. As was usual with peasants, their conversation was about their homes and farmlands.

'Brother Baraju,' said Jadu. 'Everything's destiny. Written on your forehead. Last year the sugarcane crop was so bountiful, but look at this year's—so bad we might not recover our seed money.'

'And we've had no control over that. Oh, we peasants, we can only put in our hard labour, that's all; the rest doesn't depend on us.'

'Brother, everything's beyond us. Name one thing we have control over, can you? What do the scriptures say? Work's your only religion, there's nothing beyond it! When my son fell ill last year, what did I not pledge to the gods and goddesses? How many million prayers did I offer Goddess Mangala alone? But did anything or anyone save my boy? Truly, there's nothing beyond destiny. Should my boy have survived, I wouldn't be so worried now. If he'd gone to work in Calcutta, would the paddy loan from Jagu Swain or the cash loan from Hari Mishra remain unpaid?'

'If only destiny disposed as man proposed . . .'

'Damn right, brother. Man can only propose. He can only put in his efforts, his hard work—to turn mud into gold and gold into mud!'

Baraju smiled playfully. 'Just have a look at the best example: Hari Mishra. Look at his destiny, his fate.'

'Seeing him, can we still claim virtue and righteousness exist on Earth? Sometimes I wonder if all that only exists in the printed pages of the scriptures. Hari Mishra may be a pure-blooded Brahmin, but is there any mischief he hasn't got up to? Has anyone counted how many homes he has wrecked, how many lives he has ruined? The other day, without batting an eyelid, he swore before the land settlement officer with his hand on the holy tulsi-leaf garland from the temple that some land was wrongly recorded in the name of the Jenas and actually belonged to him. He can swallow fire and nothing happens to him—he has no qualms. Why didn't his horrible heart explode when he reeled off all those lies! Look at him: is there anything he doesn't have? Wealth, manpower, cattle—you name it. Looking at him you'd think dharma has vanished from the face of Earth.'

A shudder ran through Baraju Pradhan. What, no dharma, no righteousness left on Earth! Nothing but wickedness, immorality, sin, crime and cruelty? Did humanity only value these? It was said that in primitive tribes the strong killed and devoured not only other humans but also their own wives and children, as sneakily as tomcats. Did humans still live like that today, killing or being killed? Whoever had greater power—material wealth, physical prowess or intelligence—preyed on the weak and the lowly, capturing and dismembering them, eating them and gaining weight. Was this what humans were all about? 'Don't discriminate when it comes to food, eat whatever is available, and wherever.' Didn't this line from the Bhagavat apply to humans? But didn't lack of goodness lead to the events chronicled in the Ramayana and the Mahabharata? The lack of virtue split Mother Earth in two. Hadn't that formed part of the collective human experience?

'But virtue does exist, brother,' he replied, almost shouting. 'It's always been present. Just because some people have taken to unjust and immoral ways, to unrighteousness, does not mean virtue has vanished from the face of the earth. Before we start blaming others we need to look at ourselves—aren't we all the same? Remember that in order to uphold righteousness and virtue a little squirrel pitched in to build a bridge across the ocean by ferrying sand on its back; monkeys rushed in only to be slaughtered in droves; hundreds of thousands of warriors, chieftains and kings left their wives and children and spilled their own blood on battlefields. But what are we in this village engaged in? Every family is split into two if not three factions. Fathers don't get along with sons, brothers with brothers, husbands with wives. Is it any wonder then that there are people like Hari Mishra to set you up against me, only too happy to get us to fight over something he himself will soon grab? Quite like a monkey in charge of the weighing scale, eh? The sly creature ends up eating the whole laddu! Is it fair to blame Hari Mishra? Is he the only culprit? What about us—the so-called pure and virtuous, the holy tulsi? No matter how often we bow before Goddess Mangala, we can't make a human out of a monster. Can we simply blame Hari when we ourselves are without even a semblance of virtue?'

'Brother, I couldn't agree with you more,' said Jadu. 'But all these explanations are only one side of the coin. The other side's destiny, fate. Hari Mishra's karma is strong. He's the moneylender, the landlord, the headman. The police, the officers and everyone else all eat out of his hand. Would that be possible if his destiny wasn't strong?'

'You've hit the nail on its head,' replied Baraju. 'Destiny's everything. But consider this. If there's no rain my sugarcane crop shrivels and withers—that's one kind of destiny. But creating a rift between people and then registering the land in the wrong name and making a pile of money—that's another kind of destiny. It was only because of such devilish scheming the need arose for land surveyors and revenue officers, police, lawyers and court registrars and judges. And we're left adrift on a sea without a shore. So there are two kinds of destiny. Here, in this village, our destiny is Hari Mishra, right?'

A bullock cart passed at a distance, its ungreased wheels creaking and groaning. The cart driver clucked and cracked his goad on the backs of the bullocks, occasionally belting out snatches of the song 'When Ram went for his wedding, his brother Lakshman joined the groom's merry party . . .' Baraju's words seemed like the waves of a gentle breeze wafting over the paddy seedlings.

'Too true,' answered Jadu Dalei. 'I understand completely. But somehow your words jar too, brother. Well, all right, granted Hari Mishra's rotten. But what about the officers, lawyers, and judges? Are they any good for us?'

'That depends on how fair they are. If they decide to be just, we're in luck, our karma's strong. If they choose to be unjust and nasty, our destiny's weak. But don't you see, it all begins with our own immorality in the first instance?'

'Right, brother. You said it. It's all because the world's basically unjust. What does it matter if only one or two or a

minuscule few choose to remain good when the rest don't?
The good will have no place in the midst of the bad.'

'But a million things begin with one—one, then two,
then three, then another and yet another . . . One good
person is enough to transform twenty-five wicked persons
into good. A flower spreads its fragrance all around, not just
in one direction. And the stronger the fragrance, the further
its reach.'

The grating and grinding of bullock-cart wheels receded
into the distance, along with the driver's clucking and the
cracking of his goad. Snatches of his singing could still be
heard: '. . . up above the golden platform . . . .'

*

Far away from there, in the Pradhan household, the elder
daughter-in-law was seeing to her children's breakfast. To
one she served rice puffs, to another some flattened rice,
while it was watered rice for the third. Then she picked up
a green twig to brush her teeth and proceeded to the pond
in the backyard for her bath.

Since the passing of her mother-in-law, her relationship
with the younger daughter-in-law had become severely
strained. They could no longer stand the sight of each
other, taking exception to every word and not missing a
single opportunity to be rude.

When it came to sharing the household chores, some sort
of a division of labour was in place. It had fallen to the younger
daughter-in-law to feed the cattle, clean their shed, make

cow-dung cakes and steam the paddy. The elder daughter-in-law cooked for the family and did all the rest. Neither would do any extra work: the elder woman never turned the drying paddy over, the younger wouldn't ever feed a dry twig into the oven even if the fire was about to die out.

As Hara Bou, the elder daughter-in-law, reached the pond, a few neighbours turned up one by one. Scrubbing her brass bangles with scoops of sand and mud, Mani's mother said, 'What's wrong, Hara Bou, why so late this morning?'

'What could I do? I had to grate turmeric, make mustard paste, and serve food to my children before I was free.'

Mani's mother never missed a chance to dig for more dirt. 'Couldn't the younger daughter-in-law see to your kids' breakfast?'

'Oh, she who comes from a rich family finds my children give off a foul smell! She'd much rather hole up in her bedroom chatting and laughing with her husband than look after my kids. She doesn't stir even when she sees the rice pot boiling over. Not even if you go dry in the mouth begging her to attend to such a minor chore.'

Saradi Bou, busy brushing her armlet with the bristles of her twig toothbrush, added, 'What? The young woman remains closeted with her husband in their bedroom in the morning? Would that have happened if Baraju's mother were still alive? Goodness, what horrible stuff one lives to hear!'

'That's not all, sister,' Hara Bou said. 'Even when the elder brother's home, the younger brother and his wife go overboard laughing, joking and talking loudly. A passer-by would take our house for a brothel!'

Widow Panda, in the middle of offering palmfuls of water to the sun god, pitched in: 'This is Kaliyug, my dear, the age of darkness. You'll live to see and hear of many more instances of depravity and misdemeanours as days go by. I remember, for the first thirty years of my marriage I didn't sneak a look at my husband's face in the daytime, let alone spend time with him. But these days, oh my God, people cosy up with their own younger brother's wife. Disgusting! One can't even imagine what they get up to.'

Pricking up her ears, the younger daughter-in-law heard snatches of their conversation and, pretending to attend to some chore in the backyard, came out of the house so she could hear better. When Chhakadi came home, she related all she had been able to make out, adding whatever she hadn't. What could Chhakadi say? Was he bold enough to raise the issue with his elder brother?

With no parents-in-law around, the two women took to quarrelling brazenly, each too full of herself, having no respect or consideration for the other. They fought all the time, whether sitting or standing. One day, the elder woman was sitting on the veranda. As the younger one walked by, her foot inadvertently brushed against the elder. She apologized at once, but the older one blew her top: 'Don't you take notice of human beings any longer, huh? Or have you taken to kicking people as you walk by?'

The younger woman made a face. 'Why do some people sit wherever they please?' she asked. 'Can't they find a place where they won't be in the way?'

'Adding insult to injury! A slur on top of a slap! What effrontery!'

'Why, can't one speak one's mind?' the younger one shot back. 'Nobody's at anybody else's mercy.'

There followed a regular war of words. The two women went on to produce words and phrases not to be found in any lexicon.

When the two brothers came home—Baraju after rounding up his work on the farmland and Chhakadi after watching a gypsy dance performance four miles from home—they both got the low-downs. Baraju got to hear of his younger brother's wife's flaws and shortcomings, and Chhakadi of his elder sister-in-law's misdeeds and misdemeanours.

Chhakadi patted his wife on the back. 'Way to go, woman. Give as good as you get. Word for word. That's how you win.'

But his wife made a face. 'Keep your empty words to yourself. Why do I have to put up with those wretches at all? Just because I live here? Don't I have the means to live on my own?'

She didn't know the answer to that for sure—whether she had the means. If anyone should have, it was Chhakadi, but he didn't know what exactly the situation was. So he tried to mollify her. 'Let's wait and see how it plays out, what the elder brother says and does.'

His wife was furious. 'Go cosy up to your brother and his wife. Cosy up to your precious nieces and nephew. But first separate from me.'

In the next room, while getting an earful about the younger daughter-in-law's misdeeds, Baraju realized matters had gone too far. He was sick of trying to calm his wife down; his words had failed to cut any ice in the past. Love and trust made the world move, and once they were betrayed no one could live with another—father with son, brother with brother, kings with their subjects; all relationships were in tatters. If two women in a small household couldn't get along, the relationship between the brothers would soon sour.

'Look, your perpetual quarrels and fights have made me keep away from home during the day,' he said. 'Now I'll have to think how to stay away the nights too.'

What rotten luck. 'That's the only stick you know how to dangle,' she said with a timid sigh, 'that one day you'll stop coming home, leaving your wife and children high and dry. Why instead don't you put your mind to how to put an end to the daily domestic spats and squabbles?'

But the ways Baraju suggested seemed impossible to follow. She argued back; he listened to everything she said, but in the end put the blame on her—after all, she was the elder of the two and it was up to her to set an example for the younger woman.

So it was all her fault, Hara Bou sighed. She was the one to set an example. Because she stepped into this household before the younger one did, because she became a wife and a daughter-in-law ahead of the other. She had learnt the ropes earlier. And so she was to blame. She couldn't help but make a face. 'Yes, yes, the younger one's simply waiting eagerly to follow my lead, to obey my every command, to carry out my every wish!'

'If she refuses to fall in line,' Baraju said, 'the fault's yours. Because you're the senior! If you're not getting along, the fault's more yours because you're older, you have to have more sense than her, you have to be more understanding, more patient.'

Tears running down her cheeks, Hara Bou answered, 'I knew you'd take the side of your brother and his wife. I'm no one to you, a complete stranger.'

Baraju dished out examples from the scriptures and mythology, but to no avail. His wife refused to see the light.

*

Slowly, Chhakadi's confidence in himself was growing—in his ability to look after his own affairs and believing his world from now on was confined to his wife and himself and to nobody else. His brother, his brother's wife and their children—they had all drifted away from him. His brother was someone he never stood up to or looked in the eye. The same brother who did all the backbreaking labour in the field and who had never once asked him to put in an honest day's labour.

He no longer brought presents for his nieces and nephew from the fairs he visited—no toys, no dolls, no sweets, all because his wife didn't take it kindly and would complain about it for days on end. He felt sick to the core of his heart when the kids crowded around him, asking, 'Uncle, what have you got for us?' He would remember the days when his mother was alive. How different those days were—and where had they gone? To make up for having returned home empty-handed, he would want to pick up and cuddle the children to show them he still loved them, but he stopped himself. Good God, Netramani might be watching. She wouldn't give him a moment's peace if she caught him.

*

Hara and Suna—two of Baraju's daughters—had both reached the marriageable age, considering the practice in peasant families. How long could their marriages be put off?

Preparations for Hara's wedding put her mother in high spirits. She had to collect and put everything together, from cereals and black gram balls to a comb and a wooden container for storing vermilion.

The younger sister-in-law, not having a child of her own, couldn't stand the frenzy and started neglecting her chores. Jealousy was eating her up. She was becoming more and more wilful and lackadaisical. Sometimes Hara Bou, all in a tizzy, would issue a string of commands: young lady, go scrape coconuts, stir the curry pot, do this, do that. These were to Netramani like thorns in the flesh. Damn it, she was riled up, was any of that for her to do, part of her duties?

Chhakadi had been forewarned by her too. 'If you want to help your revered brother and sister-in-law, you may as well keep away from me. Don't come near me.'

So what could the poor man do but keep away from his brother and his family. But still, there were matters he could not hide from: buying the oil, fixing the honorarium for the wedding priest, making arrangements to entertain the bridegroom's entourage. Outdoors, away from his wife's searching gaze, he discussed the planning of the wedding, but indoors he maintained a studied silence. Still there was no escape. If he ran full tilt into his wife, she, like a cobra with its hood raised high, didn't spare him. 'Why can't you relax? Why don't you lie down and rest instead of hanging around outdoors and poking your nose into the wedding preparations?'

The festive atmosphere had even the house kittens jumping for joy with their tails raised, but he wasn't allowed to be cheerful even inside his own head.

Hara's wedding was solemnized in style. She was bedecked with ornaments from head to toe. The sumptuous wedding feast drew praise from everyone. Baraju didn't stint, spending according to his worth. But far more money was spent by the bridegroom's family; they gave lavish presents—Berhampuri silk saris and gold jewellery.

*

After the wedding feast, with everyone fed and sated, Saradi Bou and Widow Panda sat down with the younger daughter-in-law to roll paan.

'Young lady,' Saradi Bou began. 'Where's your new sari, why aren't you wearing it?'

Netramani made a face. 'A new sari for me, aunt? Why, is this my first homecoming or what?'

'What nonsense, young woman. There's a wedding in the family. Even the humble drummers have new clothes. Didn't Baraju get new clothes for his own family members?'

Widow Panda, her eyes swivelling around the room, snorted. 'Oh, don't take her seriously, Saradi Bou. She's fibbing.' She got up and pulled out a new red sari from the loft. 'Here's her new sari.'

Old Saradi Bou, leader of the village gossips, had seen the weddings of the Chowdhuries, the landlords of Jenapur, which were billed the most lavish of all and before which all others paled into insignificance, and knew the names of all the ornaments and had seen every variety of silk. She ran her fingers over Netramani's new red sari and turned up her nose. 'Woe is me, this is just a Godavari sari of the most inferior quality. The colour's bound to run.'

'But I saw Hara Bou wearing one exactly like this,' Widow Panda remarked.

'You don't get it, do you?' said Saradi Bou, dropping her voice. 'Where, in which scripture, is it written that both daughters-in-law will have similar saris? The elder daughter-in-law, who has had it good, can't be put in the same bracket as the younger daughter-in-law. Tell me, whose daughter's wedding is being celebrated? Much has been spent on the bride's ornaments, and her saris were ordered from Behrampur. Couldn't a sari of better quality be bought for the younger daughter-in-law?'

Panda Widow stole a glance at Netramani with a sly smile. 'Is that why this young woman's peevish?'

As if the lady in question was not present in their midst, Saradi Bou replied, 'Now, what kind of an observation is that? Why should the younger daughter-in-law sulk over a trifle? Doesn't she have enough good saris to keep her from getting depressed? Hasn't she had a taste of the good life— good saris, good food and all the rest?'

'Nobody's denying that,' the widow said. 'Who doesn't know the kind of family she hails from? Her father's so well off. Of course she isn't dying for a good sari. Didn't you see how she went and changed into an ordinary sari the moment she finished blessing the newly-weds?'

Netramani bristled with pride. 'You know what, aunt? When my elder sister was married, saris of this quality were given to the wives of the barber and the washerman.'

Saradi Bou clucked in agreement. 'Who doesn't know that? We understand you well enough to know you wouldn't have a craving for a sari in the way a witch does for a new-born baby!'

But Saradi Bou had no idea the kind of family Netramani was from.

5

Hari Mishra was the village headman. He had managed to obtain this position of authority by paying a large quantity of high-quality paddy and ghee to the powers that be. Over the years, thanks to his machinations, he had been able to take over the properties of quite a few hapless widows and waifs, whose lives he had successfully wrecked.

His dislike for Baraju Pradhan was immense, which was of course understandable. The man was a thorn in his flesh, an obstruction, an impediment to his schemes, foiling many of them. Moreover, Mishra had suffered nothing but loss of face, embarrassment and humiliation at his hands, not only in his own village but in several nearby ones too. Baraju was invariably the first person sought out to adjudicate land and family disputes; it was he who was called upon to lead the team of five elders to settle disputes amicably, without the parties having to run to the law courts. Hari Mishra stood to lose because of these interventions. If a dispute went to court, the enquiry reports to be submitted could be doctored and good amounts of money could be made. Almost any

report could be suitably tailored: just take your pick—
one for a quarter-rupee or one for a half? But because
of Baraju, Mishra's business had taken a hit. He had far
fewer opportunities. Baraju had opened the people's eyes.
In a couple of important disputes in which Mishra could
have made a tidy sum from both sides, Baraju had become
involved and sorted them out to the satisfaction of the
parties concerned. How long could Mishra take it? The
fellow was a bloody peasant who might not be able to
spell his father's name, but the amount of meddling he did
in matters best left to Mishra was unacceptable.

Mishra was picking at a bit of betel nut lodged between
his teeth when he noticed Chhakadi heading towards his
shop with a bag.

'Chhakadi, son, is that you?' he said. 'Our sister Akhai's
son! Come over here, my boy. Come and sit with me
awhile and tell me all about the wedding expenses. How
much did you have to fork out from your own pocket?'

'Uncle, why ask me?' Chhakadi said. 'You attended
the ceremony, you were there all the time, you joined in
the festivities, so you must have a good idea of how much
everything cost.'

'Hah, hah—what did I see? Was I able to go into the
details? I was merely a guest, a spectator at the wedding like
the others. I was there only to enjoy the feast, I had no eyes
for anything else.'

'But why are you asking me, Uncle?'

'Who else, if not you, huh? You're family, Baraju's
own brother, you must have handled the cash, you must

have first-hand knowledge of the goings-on. Would I go and ask Chinta Hadi the scavenger instead?'

'Uncle,' Chhakadi became grave. 'Truth to tell, I'm no better than Chinta Hadi.'

'What a thing to say, my boy! How can you say you're no better than Chinta Hadi? For god's sake, you aren't anything like the village scavenger!'

'Since you're asking, Uncle, let me tell you I wasn't in on the wedding plans or expenses. I saw nothing, I did nothing, I know nothing.'

'I don't buy that. But if it's true, it doesn't reflect well on Baraju. What kind of an elder brother is he? After all, you're his own younger brother, born of the same mother, and living under the same roof.'

'Uncle, don't blame him. He's not responsible.' Chhakadi's entire ire was directed at his sister-in-law.

'Come on, don't talk like a child. You want me to believe Baraju's above reproach? That his wife's to blame? What do you take me for—a dimwit, huh?'

'But that's all I can repeat, over and over again. My brother . . .'

'Yes, yes, we're talking about your brother. Now you might think no end of him, but do go and ask around to find out what other people think. Two brothers live together under the same roof but one doesn't know anything about the household income, expenditures and savings?'

'But, Uncle,' Chhakadi said emphatically. 'I don't distrust my brother for a moment.'

Mishra became a little subdued. Sometimes honesty did triumph over falsehood. 'Come on,' he said. 'That's not what I was suggesting. All I'm saying is you don't have to swallow whatever you're told as the gospel truth, not even the words of your own guru. Check things for yourself. Baraju's a good man and everyone's understandably full of praise for him, that's right. But he too has his share of faults—that's all I'm saying. He has a childless younger brother who trusts him wholeheartedly. So why can't he return at least a quarter of that trust? Never mind that the younger brother is an irresponsible brat, that he doesn't do a spot of work for the family. As an elder brother, has Baraju ever entrusted ten rupees to his younger brother and asked him to do a bit of shopping? Did he ask this younger brother to sit with him and go over the wedding expenses? Would that have strengthened the brotherly trust, or weakened it?'

'Uncle, since you mention it,' Chhakadi replied truthfully, 'my brother did ask me to keep the accounts, to go buy the provisions for the wedding. But I told him all that was beyond me, that he must look for someone else. So he went and caught hold of his brother-in-law.'

Hari Mishra clapped his hands together. 'That's it. He did seek somebody's help, didn't he? Why a brother-in-law, when you've a younger brother of your own, eh? That's something I'd positively feel let down about.'

Chhakadi had never been someone with a strong mind—he was easy to influence, and for once Hari Mishra's words hit home. It occurred to him he was playing second fiddle, whether in or outside the home. 'Uncle,' he said with a sigh, 'these problems will remain as long as brothers are living together under the same roof. Once they separate, they won't even make good neighbours; they're too taken up with their own problems.'

'Separate? But why? There's absolutely no cause for a split between you and your brother, is there? Don't be childish!'

'I'm not being childish, Uncle. Not for a moment. But I don't know how long we can carry on living under the same roof. On the surface we might seem together, but in reality we've already fallen apart. Our relationship now has the taste of curry that's burnt.'

'Come on, my boy, that's all nonsense. You two aren't old enough for a family partition. You're still a teenager— given to good food and good clothes, you seek out different people to keep yourself amused. If you wish, I could make you a member of the local council.'

'No, Uncle. I won't accept any position until I separate from my brother.'

'Ah, don't go on like that, son. Forget about separating. Look, nobody's saying you can't—of course you can, but you're far too young and callow to look after yourself. Aren't you?'

'Uncle,' Chhakadi laughed, 'Tell me, will you provide me with my meals if I do nothing but sit in your courtyard?'

'Come on, what kind of talk is that? What don't you have that you would end up living at someone else's mercy? Hey, you're Shyam Pradhan's son after all! What have you reduced yourself to? No, that won't do, I tell you, it simply won't. Why do you have to beg for my help? You're like a son to me. If you wish, I could loan you three hundred rupees tomorrow morning itself—take it and start a business of your own, open a shop, live off the profit and pay me back the principal in easy instalments. I'd consider my money well-spent if I could use a bit of it for the welfare of a son of Shyam Pradhan. Shyam was someone to be reckoned with, people looked up to him, they valued his views and respected his opinion. What I don't like is that his son has to roam around like some sort of ghost. How can anyone stand the sight? Not me, for one, oh no.'

The whole village knew the truth about just how deep Hari Mishra's goodwill towards Shyam Pradhan went. Hari Mishra would advise someone to trim the hedge separating his piece of land from his neighbour's ('Don't you see the fellow's trying to encroach upon your land? Why don't you shave off a bit of the hedge, huh?'), and, if the other party objected, he would order both parties to make deposits of 500 rupees so that the claims could be verified, measurements could be made afresh and a proper demarcating hedge could be put in place. Half the money collected went into Hari Mishra's own coffers for his role. But the moment he got wind of it, Shyam Pradhan would intervene and get the feuding parties to sit together and sort out the rift, no matter how ticklish it was. And all without having to spend a single paisa.

Suppose two women went to the village pond together for a bath and one of them lost an earring, missing it only after returning home. She would confront her companion to give it back, because she was the only likely person to have scooped it up. If a matter such as this were to reach Hari Mishra's ears, he would summon the first woman's husband or guardian and give him an earful: 'Hey, are you planning to run me out of here? Drum me out of my position as the village council headman? This incident involves theft, a police enquiry and a lawsuit. You might be happy just to get back the stolen jewellery and then think the whole incident was behind you, but who'd take care of the police case? The police would swoop down on the village and catch not only the thief but you too. And poor me as well. For not reporting the case to the police station in the first instance, for trying to hush it up. Are you out to sink me?' The poor victim wouldn't know what to say. Then Hari Mishra would soften a bit and advise him: 'Never mind, go and give the village chowkidar a little bribe and make a contribution to the village temple fund, and remember that the chowkidar and the village deity are not on the same footing and cannot be treated alike; in fact, one is as different from the other as east is from west.' And he, Hari Mishra, couldn't be lumped in with the village chowkidar either. Anyone who made that mistake had hell to pay. So Mishra made something from every transaction. As the saying goes, he who raises the wick of the oil lamp gets his fingers greased. Hari Mishra never let a single opportunity pass him by. 'What're you saying?' he would say, putting a spin on the matter. 'Seems like terrible times are upon us again! You dare spirit away an earring off your companion's ear while you're both taking a bath! If things come to such a pass, people will start stealing the kohl from one another's eyes!'

Keeping people of his kind in mind, Shyam Pradhan would comment: 'We're poor folks, our gaze is always fixed on trifles—a bottle gourd or a pumpkin. We'll always remain the petty thieves we are. But these big people, like the village council headman or zamindar or moneylender, they're brigands and bandits in comparison. They scare the wits out of you in broad daylight in the name of the law, drag you through the corridors of the courts and bleed you until you become worse than a beggar in the street. Just as there are man-eating tigers and crocodiles, there are man-eating headmen too. And like the tigers and crocodiles, they care two hoots for the law and the justice system; they couldn't care less. It's in their blood. And as the saying goes, a man's nature never changes during his lifetime, just as it's the nature of pigs to wallow in filth.'

Hari Mishra was nothing if not a shining example of this—and right in front of the people's eyes. He might have been born a Brahmin, but his nature was worse than a Chandal corpse-burner's. He was like a fisherman upset at seeing a river teeming with fish when he didn't have his fishing net, or a gypsy ruing every missed opportunity of bringing down a bird in flight because he was without his catapult. He always had an eye out for some helpless widow, or an orphan who hadn't come of age, or anyone who had a lovely coconut grove next to his and which he wanted to make his own. Or someone whose tiny slice of a mango grove was right next to his and the man had fallen sick—if the poor man were to die, his widow would have to sell it off to Mishra for a song.

Mishra would have driven everyone out of the village if he could have. He would have loved for every inch of land, gardens and groves to become his own, for all the inhabitants to become his slaves, his farmhands and labourers. This was the dream that obsessed him, awake or asleep. Surely the prospect of being the victim of a ferocious beast was far more inviting. A man who was forever dreaming of dispossessing everyone around of every inch of their land was far more dangerous any day than a tiger or a crocodile.

'People often claim,' Shyam Pradhan would say, 'it's the poor who finally become deceitful, small-time thieves, mischief-makers and bad elements; apparently it's the have-nots who corrupt and spoil the haves, the rich. But does the bird ever corrupt and spoil the hunter or the fish the fisherman? Just as we take cattle out to graze, the rich take us out to the pastures—in their eyes we're neither women nor cows! We can't open our mouths even if we're given ten or twelve lashes across our bare backs. How then do we poor sods corrupt the rich, the wise and the wily? Do folks who can't even boil a bunch of greens matter in the scheme of things? Do their words have any weight? Unheard of, if you ask me.'

That was the kind of friendship Hari Mishra had shared with Shyam Pradhan. And now Shyam's offspring Baraju was trying to step into his father's shoes. Why, milk would still drip from the lad's cheeks if they were pressed, but he too was trying to undermine Hari Mishra!

6

Baraju could see the domestic squabbles and quarrels were growing by the day. Not a moment of peace—home felt worse than the cremation ground. People at home were fighting just as much as the crows, vultures, dogs and jackals. And over the smallest thing. Not a moment of respite.

At home Chhakadi maintained a thin veneer of respect for his elder brother, but once out of doors missed no opportunity to badmouth him. His grievances were many: his elder brother had held his daughter's wedding but had he told him how much he had spent? Where had the money come from? Couldn't he have consulted his younger brother?

The two brothers had mentally drifted apart, so far apart that any outward show of togetherness was meaningless; nevertheless it still helped. The thread had been broken and couldn't be made whole again, even if the pieces could still be knotted together.

Meanwhile, if the younger daughter-in-law stumbled, she blamed it on the elder daughter-in-law, on the money she had spent on the wedding. Once separated, she wouldn't have to share her wealth with anyone or let them eat into it.

The elder daughter-in-law too was ready to wage war not against just one Netramani but against five like her. That slip of a girl wouldn't get the better of her, would she?

So what was to be done? Baraju thought hard. How to restore peace at home? But no matter how much he thought about it he couldn't find a solution. Would he then formally separate from his brother? Quite a few families in the village had split up but still continued on good terms. As many partitions, went the saying, as there are brothers in a family. If both families could then live in peace, wasn't a partition worth considering? What was the point in living together in perpetual bickering and bitterness, wriggling like worms in the same hole? Since they were not of the same mind, perhaps it would be much better to live apart. It was one thing to have a partition when the brothers still loved one another, quite another when they no longer saw eye to eye. It would be better if he and Chhakadi split when they were still on talking terms. But, oh God, that was simply unthinkable! Chhakadi was just a silly little boy, whom he had carried in his arms until the other day and had dinned sense into his head when he was being stubborn and adamant. Now that he was back to being foolish again, where was his, Baraju's, fabled patience? When Chhakadi was a child, it had been so easy to divert his attention by pointing to a crow or a tree, but what could he point to now? He remembered their father's last words to him: 'Chhakadi's a silly boy, so you see to it no wall crops up in the middle of this home, no ridge across the paddy lands!' How Baraju's eyes had welled up with tears! A few fat drops had rolled down his cheeks. Nobody had ever seen him cry as much he had that day.

So from that brother he would now separate—divide the few head of cattle, the pots and pans, farmland, vegetable patch, everything half-and-half? Would he be able to show his face in the village afterwards? What would people say, what? So this was who Baraju was with all his big talk! Was this finally the measure of the man? Why, no better than any other ordinary soul!

The more he thought about it, the less he seemed likely to arrive at a decision. He had sat on the council of elders in many villages to sort out disputes and had saved so many families from litigation and lawsuits, but when it came to resolving the discord raging in his own home, he didn't know what to do. The two wives might be at each other's throats, but Chhakadi hadn't raised the issue, not yet, so why should he? Damn it, he couldn't humiliate the silly boy by doing that!

He blamed everyone in the family—his wife, his brother, his sister-in-law, but most of all himself. It was his fault the most because he was the head of the family. What had he done to douse the raging flames? Why had he been like a block of wood, a ghost, all this time? Of course he was most to blame! If the Pradhan family was now coming apart at the seams, he was the one responsible; people would be entirely right to hold him more accountable than his brother.

In the last few days, Chhakadi had become involved in the women's quarrels. Three times he had threatened

violence against Baraju's wife. Baraju had to put up with all
of this—who else if not he?

The two women were at the root of the problem; it was
they who started the bickering. If they were quiet, Chhakadi,
being a man, wouldn't start a fight. Even between the two
women, it was hard to determine who began it, who stoked
the fire and who then jumped into the fray. If only one of
them had the sense to remain silent while the other ranted
and raged. One hand doesn't clapping make. That was
right. If only his wife, Hara Bou, the elder daughter-in-law,
had the sense to be reasonable, there would be no fights,
no feuds. And who would the elder woman listen to? Her
husband, obviously! If he couldn't bring her back on the
rails, what good was he as a husband?

This line of thinking lifted his mood. There seemed the
possibility of a solution, the glimmer of hope he had been
waiting for. Could he not bring just one simple woman
back onto the straight path?

'There's something I need to talk to you about,' Baraju
said to his wife.

Something to talk to her about? she wondered. Her
husband had something to discuss with her! Were the gods
smiling down on them this morning? What on earth did
he want to talk to her about? About how frogs spawn? Her
heart seemed to brim over with happiness. How many
times in the past she had taken care to dress up—rub a paste
of turmeric and oil into her skin, comb her hair to a shine,
put kohl in her eyes and vermilion on her forehead so her
husband would take notice of her? But she had seen his

face, still and thundery as a pumpkin. She never had the good fortune of hearing a sweet word from him. And today the same old taciturn man was telling her he wanted to talk to her. Only benevolent Providence could have ordained such a stroke of good luck!

She stared at him in silence, not a word issuing from her lips.

'Tell me,' Baraju said. 'All this endless unpleasantness in the family—will it ever end, or will it go on and on?'

'Why don't you tell me how to end it? Who's picking the quarrels—she or me?' She was quick to sulk. Baraju was always siding with his brother's wife, was always finding fault with his own, was always blaming her for everything.

'It'll never come to an end if all that matters is finding out who started it,' he said.

'Whether the feuds come to an end or not, I can no longer live with her under the same roof.'

'Then partition's the only way out. There's no other solution, is there?'

'Whether you want a partition or you want to go on living together in perfect harmony, I absolutely refuse to take her cruel words and taunts any more.'

Baraju wondered if the hill of hurt feelings and grievances pressing down on his wife's heart would easily be removed. It was clear from what she was hinting at that she longed for a partition, but she wasn't able to come out with it outright, in so many words—she would never dare. 'Don't you know I hate murky waters?' he said, his lips quivering and eyes sparking. 'Be plain with me.'

Hara Bou quailed at his sudden change; she broke out in a cold sweat. What manner of a man had destiny arranged for her? Who knew what he would do now? 'You're riled up for nothing. Am I the only one around to look after the whole family? To see to everything?'

'Lies! Why are you telling lies?' Baraju exploded. 'Do you really attend to every little chore around the house? Does the younger daughter-in-law not lend a hand, never help?'

She knew tears wouldn't melt her husband's heart— it was made of stone, cast in iron. On the contrary, the slightest lie could set him off; maybe it already had. He had once stopped taking his meals at home for two straight days because she had told him a little lie. Just a little lie. A tiny little lie. And what lies don't people tell! 'Never mind. What she does or doesn't do around the house matters little. But what have my poor children done to her to make her so rude and mean to them? Day in and day out too.'

'But the children don't seem to have come to any harm for all that!'

It was Hara Bou's turn to flare up. 'Goodness! Don't you teach me the noble ways, no sir. I don't want them. I'm ready to live apart with my children.'

'Fair enough. If you're prepared to live apart with your children, then leave this place. Just don't expect me to be there with you.'

Good God, she thought. Did this man not feel anything for his own flesh and blood? She broke down in tears. 'Is that the most unpleasant thing you can threaten me with? The worst threat you can hang over my head?'

But Baraju was as unmoved as if made of lead, without one bit of tenderness in him. 'Listen up. Family quarrels are never resolved through tears and angry words.'

'Quarrels in this house will never cease,' she shot back.

'Fine,' he said, walking off. 'Go on quarrelling to your heart's content.'

He walked away quietly, like a very polite boy, like an obedient pupil, without another word.

After he left, his wife came to her senses. Only the mother of a deaf and dumb child knows what her child is trying to say. What had she done! How could she have behaved like a witch and let him walk off without lunch? The poor man had been out since early morning making the rounds of his fields without a bath or breakfast.

Tears streamed down her cheeks. How loving he had sounded when he said he wanted to have a word with her. Little had she anticipated that these were the words he had ready for her, or that they would end up with him walking away in high dudgeon. Of late she had been so guarded, so circumspect, ever mincing her words, but to what avail had all that been? When it had most mattered, she had floundered and failed and been found lacking. Why didn't she simply drop dead?

They had drifted apart, and what wife wouldn't be upset about that? She felt her anger once again building up against her brother-in-law and his wife—it was because of them she couldn't speak her mind and had behaved with her husband as if she weren't his wife but his sister-in-law. They had drifted apart, no longer able to reach out to each other; their words had become like poison to one another. Why and how had it come to this? How did it ever come to this? What oppressive weight seemed to have settled on their hearts like a mountain? There was no longer a single moment of happiness at home, day or night.

Surely somebody had cast an evil eye on them. Undoubtedly. Surely, surely. And it must have been that witch of a younger sister-in-law. She must have been the one to have cast a spell. Who else! Who else didn't have anything better to do? Never mind, oh never mind, she, Hara Bou, wouldn't take it lying down. No, she would give back as good as she got. She would vent all her bottled-up anger on the younger woman, God save her. She didn't have to remain Ghana Parida's dear docile daughter or the loving little wife of Baraju Pradhan! Enough was enough. 'Moti,' she called out to her daughters. 'Suna! Go look for your father. This enemy was born for me!'

Moti and Suna scurried out to go looking for their father. They found him stretched out on the platform at Goddess Mangala's temple, not even a threadbare towel underneath him, not far from the narrow village path fringed by screw pine bushes on either side. There was a gnarled marigold plant in the middle of the courtyard and a little blackbird was hopping around it trying to perch on its fragile leaves. A little distance away was Baraju's plot of sugarcane; the crop seemed healthy because of the care he had given it. From time to time his eyes roamed over the field he had pinned much hopes on. The amount of trouble he had taken to cultivate it, the amount of sweat he had poured into the enterprise!

The day was done, the shadows were coming on. But in Baraju's home everyone had gone without food, just because he had refused to have his. The faces of his two children, out in the sun the whole day looking for him, had become dark.

But Baraju finally came home in their company. What else could he do? If he didn't take his meals nobody else in the family would, and he hated to make them go without food. How long could he let them starve? But, on the other hand, if he gave in now, he would never be able to achieve anything. Some people went to great lengths to achieve what they wanted, doing arduous penance and living off blades of grass. Would he, Baraju, content himself with the little he had attempted and meekly submit to defeat? Would he let Hara Bou win just because she had gone on a hunger strike? If she won, she would remain the quarrelsome harridan she had become of late, and the family fights would go on and on. Even if there was a family partition, the two women wouldn't accept it with an open mind. What a pity people should separate just because they didn't get along with one another, because they couldn't change their nature. Good and bad existed within all human beings—people carried both, gods and demons, within them; the gods were forever at loggerheads with the demons. Sometimes one side won, sometimes the other. When good triumphed over evil, humans were worshipped as gods—they became immortal, an inspiration to others to tread the path of virtue and goodness. When evil triumphed, the same humans became thugs, bandits, thieves and murderers. But, going by the increase in fighting in every family in every village of late, evil seemed to be enlarging its empire; the demons seemed to be winning against the gods. All the wars between the gods and the demons described in the Ramayana and the Mahabharata were nothing if not wars between good and evil. The same thing was happening now and would continue until the end of time.

After realizing that, would he, Baraju, still choose to lose to the demons? Just because Hara Bou was crying her eyes out and refusing to eat? Wouldn't the demons become stronger and finally destroy his family? No, he was made of sterner stuff. He wouldn't give in so easily. It was in a battle like this that Lord Ram—a prince, a mighty king's son, no less—had defeated his own father and left his home and hearth and his wife. If narrow affection and attachments were in control, then evil would simply win. Take the example of the Pandava brothers. What sufferings did they not undergo? In the end, all scriptures and Puranas were about this one thing: the triumph of good and the defeat of evil, the gods upstaging the demons.

Now the same demons were wrecking the Pradhan family. They were on the rise, ruling over all the family members—Baraju, Chhakadi and their wives. To defeat the demons, Lord Ram chose to put up with the pangs of separation from his loving old father and subjected his wife to untold suffering in the forest; the Pandavas too had left their kingdom behind, and their wife Draupadi had to put up with the bitterest of humiliations and deprivations. What was Baraju compared to them? Not even a speck of dust! Couldn't he take his little share of misery and sorrow in his stride? Let his wife starve, go without food for five days or more, let the kids cry out in hunger. He wouldn't forsake the gods and rush into the inviting arms of the demons. He would stoutly refuse to bend. Was he without love for his wife, then? Of course not. But he only loved her for the good in her, not for the evil. The love of evil was not true love; just the opposite. He would brim over with love for his wife, but only after he had purged her of her vileness. Because he loved her he wished the very best for her. If she didn't realize what was good for herself or where her strength lay, wasn't it the duty of her husband to make her understand? It was for this reason precisely they didn't see eye to eye. Different points of view separated them; they could never agree. Medicines are always bitter and no one, no matter how ill, enjoys taking them. But aren't they appreciated after recovery?

Baraju went back home and sat down to his meal, although his heart wasn't in it. His mind was still quite troubled; he continued to worry about how to reduce his unhappiness at home.

His eyes no longer glinted with joy and happiness, and he wondered why solving the little problem afflicting his family was beyond him. Other men led nations and empires, but he had failed to lead even his small family.

The change in his behaviour didn't escape his wife's notice. She saw her husband was fast drifting away; he was no longer fond of his home and children. One glance at his bowl and she knew he was eating much less.

Pushed to her limits, she blurted out: 'Look at the man who's taken to roaming around without his regular meals. Surely some witch of a barren widow has cast a spell on him!'

The younger daughter-in-law shot out of her room. 'Hey, what did you call me—a widow?'

Baraju decided against the nap he had been planning and walked out.

Once he had done that, he decided not to return home this time.

A day passed, then a couple and then five. He resolutely stayed away. His wife sent word around to look for him, but he seemed to have vanished into thin air. No one had any news of him.

'Goodness, Hara Bou,' said Saradi Bou. 'What have you done to yourself? You've become as thin as a dried fish! And what came over Baraju? He was such a nice man!'

Tears rolled down poor Hara Bou's eyes. 'Just my rotten luck! Even a good man turns bad in my company.'

'Stop crying, woman. Baraju will be back soon, I'm telling you.'

Hara Bou was racked by convulsive sobs. 'Oh, why am I not dead and gone? Do I have any confidence he'll be back?'

Seeing their mother in tears, the children too broke out wailing. 'Mother's crying,' the youngest one began blubbering. 'Ma's crying.'

Hara Bou gave up hope Baraju would return anytime soon. How careful and cautious she had been in his presence, always keeping her mouth shut even as her blood boiled! But in one unguarded moment her miserable little tongue had betrayed her. If only she could get hold of a little poison to put an end to her miserable life!

'Don't carry on so, Hara Bou,' Saradi Bou said. 'There's more to it all. A calm and cool man like your husband would never be so abrupt and thoughtless unless there was something else. Who turns his back on wife and children just like that?'

'You said it,' Hara Bou agreed, recovering a little. 'He simply upped and left, just because I refused to listen to him.'

Saradi Bou's voice dropped. 'But don't you worry. Of all witch doctors the best I have come across is Saria Ojha; there's none better than him. Once he gave a woman such a potion that her man who was missing for over seven or eight years came home inside of two days!'

'Where can I find Saria Ojha, where does he live? How do I get in touch with him?'

'Woman, who's telling you to go to him yourself? What are friends for? And it's not going to cost you an arm or a leg, either. All it takes is seven cakes, roasted on one side only, seven lamps filled with pure ghee, seven bunches of holy *duba* grass . . .'

Saradi Bou laid out the list and took the money from Hara Bou to arrange everything.

7

Dusk again descended on the village. The cattle made their way home, the birds winged their way back to their nests. In the middle of the vast stretch of paddy fields someone was shouting, 'Come home, Navina. Where the hell are you?' The young daughters and daughters-in-law in the peasant families placed lighted wicks at the altar of the sacred tulsi plants growing on raised clay platforms. Wisps of smoke curled up from the thatched roofs of houses.

In Chhakadi's shop, which had recently opened to sell betel leaves and nuts and tobacco, business was brisk, with the bustle of customers coming and going.

'Boy, get this paddy weighed. I need to buy a couple of things.'

'Uncle Chhakadi, weigh my basket of paddy too.'

'Hey, I want a plug of tobacco.'

'Chhakadi, son, give me a box of matches.'

'Hurry up, I can hear my little one bawling.'

Chhakadi found all this taxing and confusing, just too much to cope with. 'Woman, little do I care whether your child's bawling or dying!' Clearly, the pressure of

74

handling so many customers at the same time was getting to him.

'Hey, give me back my paddy,' the woman shouted back. 'I came here to buy something, not to put up with your nasty temper.'

'Take it back, then. Go on, take it away.'

Someone else piped up. 'Hurry up, boy. I don't have all day. Attend to me. And for god's sake, stop picking on the poor customers!'

'Hey, son, look at these tobacco leaves. They're so musty. How old are they?'

'Chhakadi, my boy, hurry up and give me two bidis. I was about to heat water to feed my cattle when I remembered I'd run out.'

'Hang on.' Chhakadi exploded, his voice hoarse from talking incessantly. 'How many hands do you think I have? My throat's gone dry too. All right now, Sania Ma, tell me what do you want to buy.'

'Some leaves of tobacco.' She thrust forward a bowl of paddy.

'Why don't you take over as salesman?' Chhakadi said with rising irritation, pushing her bowl away.

'Grow some more hands boy,' Sania Ma said, 'if you can't make do with two. I told you my child was crying when I left home, and I've been waiting here since sunset. How many hours have passed since—two? Don't you have a drop of compassion left in you? Never mind, take this paddy and give me some betel leaves and nuts, a lump of *catchu* and a couple of tobacco leaves . . .'

'All for the tiny amount of paddy you've got? It's not worth a paisa, but you want to buy up the whole shop, eh?'

'What's bitten you today, boy? Until now this was enough for everything I needed! Stop making a fuss and give me what I want.'

Poor Chhakadi—he hadn't relished the idea of wading through mud and squelch day in day out, so he had shied away from agriculture and working on the land. Running a shop had seemed a better option. His brother, Baraju, had helped out with some funds too. From Baraju's point of view, it was better for the good-for-nothing to run a business than to sit idle.

But part of the money Chhakadi got from his brother, he had already spent getting his wife's anklets repaired. So he had less money for goods. Sales didn't pick up— they didn't really amount to much—and his wife's requirements for betel leaves and nuts had to be met out of the stock. In the beginning, Suna and Moti had turned up to take things from the shop for free, but their mother had stopped them after a while. 'We'd better buy what we need from Siddhi Sahu,' she told them. 'Chhakadi might be generous and might give you a paisa's worth of merchandise for free, but his wife will keep going on about it being worth twelve annas.'

Forget about making a tidy profit, poor Chhakadi was finding it difficult to recover his investment—that's how sound his business was. But what other options did he have?

*

People seemed to drop in at his shop more to sit and gossip than to buy anything. Hari Mishra was among the regulars. He was angry with Baraju beyond words; his blood boiled at the sight of the man, and he fondly hoped the two brothers would split up sooner rather than later. That would stop Baraju from showing off, Hari Mishra thought. Then we'll see how a man who hasn't been able to paper over the cracks in his own family will go round trying to iron out other people's disputes! We'll see what explanation he'll offer when asked why he's failed in his own family. That's when we'll be able to take the measure of the man. Trying to be a broker of peace all around while his own home's being rocked by a rift? We'll see how he'll prevent having his homestead, household goods and cooking utensils and cattle and land divided up!

'Hey, godson,' Mishra said, dropping in at Chhakadi's shop one evening. 'How's business?'

Chhakadi rolled out a palm-leaf mat for him. 'Sit down, Uncle.'

After Hari Mishra had made himself comfortable, Chhakadi began to prepare a paan for the old man. Business hours ended rather early in the evening, within the first hour after sunset; whoever turned up after that did so only to gossip.

'It's good you opened this little shop,' commented Hari Mishra.

'Did he even seriously give it any thought in the beginning?' asked Dharama Das.

Hari Mishra was a squinter—a 'sun-squinter'. In the company of ten people, each would think he was looking directly at him. If Mishra looked straight ahead, his eyeballs rolled to the right; if he turned to his left, his eyes stared straight ahead. He now tried to focus on Dharama Das. 'But tell me, did Chhakadi steal money from anyone to set up his shop? He had his father's money to get started.'

'Actually, Uncle,' Chhakadi corrected him, 'Father didn't leave a single coin behind. When he was dying he said all he was leaving us was dharma and righteousness!'

'Oh yes, I heard that too. But if your parents didn't leave behind a nest egg, did Baraju fork out funds from his personal savings? And what do people have to say about that? Left on our own, we tend to believe what we get to hear.'

'I don't know if he did, Uncle. But I was very much present when my parents passed; I saw them as they took their last breath, but I didn't hear either of them mention any wealth.'

'Ha, ha. You didn't. Nor did you bother to find out, did you? All someone as innocent as you wanted was to live off your parents' charity while it lasted! What do you say, Dharama?'

'No, sir,' said Dharama. 'Every bit of money for the shop came from Baraju. And he borrowed it all from Guna Parida.'

'You trying to tell me what's what, eh, Dharama? Come on, I knew Shyam Pradhan through and through. And his wife too. I've also seen Baraju since he was a baby.'

'But sir, we've never seen the slightest wrongdoing on Baraju's part . . .'

'Aw, shut up.' Mishra was suddenly very angry. 'You dare contradict me, man? What do you know that you dare go against Hari Mishra? Well, Chhakadi my boy . . .'

'I couldn't agree with you more, Uncle. Even the gods fail to see through human deceit.'

'That's it, that's just it. It takes an intelligent man to catch on. Now this Dharama Das—since when does he think he can sit and chat with us like an equal? In the past, did people like him dare talk, let alone sit with us? People like him went out at first light to till the fields with only cold rice-water for breakfast! But what have the times come to? A low-caste man no longer bothers about how he talks to his superiors!'

Dharama Das shrank back a little. 'No sir,' he said, trying to placate Mishra. 'I had no intention of contradicting you . . .'

'Shut up, wise man,' Hari Mishra barked. 'All right, let's, for the sake of argument, accept it was Baraju who forked out the funds. Wasn't the entire amount from their joint property? If he doled out a little out of the common income to his younger brother, what big act of charity was that, what's the big deal about that?'

Chhakadi tried to pacify the old man. 'Uncle, what does Dharama know of the affairs of our household? Why take him seriously?'

But Dharama was nothing if not an obstinate mule, always free and frank with his opinions. He might receive a few slaps and blows for them, but he would never pass up an opportunity to air them openly. True, he didn't have the temerity to join issue with the likes of Hari Mishra, but he wasn't shy about taking on callow young fellows like Chhakadi. 'Oh yes, we do have a fair idea of how much you yourself know of your own family affairs! You can't even distinguish between the image of a god and the wooden platform it's placed on. Will you be able to get back the investment in this shop?'

'Aw, be quiet, man. Keep your mouth shut in the presence of a highly respectable man like our Uncle Hari here. We know what your precious words of wisdom are worth!'

'Speak softly you,' Dharama replied. 'Keep a leash on your tongue. Are you going to hit me or what? Look here, this Dharama might be low caste, he might not own any land or house or gold which need protecting, but you can't stop him from speaking the truth, can you? You might even slap him around a bit, but then he's been used to that from childhood. Beatings and scolding he's had aplenty! But he's no thief or rogue that you can lock him up in jail.'

What the hell! Hari Mishra flew into a rage. The untouchable moron had the audacity to talk big in his presence? But then he was nothing if not an inveterate fool, and he, Hari Mishra, had thrashed him many a time in the past to drive that home. 'Boy, has your back been itching badly this evening?'

But Dharama was way past caring. He knew the worst outcome of bandying words with Hari Mishra would be some slaps and blows. What did that matter? In the normal course of the day, they didn't; but the prospect was certainly not inviting now, in the depths of the night, so to speak. 'Is that all you're capable of?' he said, getting to his feet. 'Threatening to beat me? To beat, scold and scare me, to run me out of the village? What does that matter to me? I'm a farmhand, I'll be able to keep body and soul together wherever I go. As long as I'm able to move my hands and legs, I'll find work! I'm not growing wealthier by the day, with riches I need to take care of and protect. I've nothing that needs looking after. Still, people like you wouldn't let a pumpkin vine grow on the thatched roof of my house. I really don't see why I should stick to this damn village. Anybody will snap up a farmhand like me wherever I go . . .'

'Go, man. Scram.' Hari Mishra was livid. 'It's already late in the evening and I don't relish the prospect of polluting myself by giving you a good hiding right now. I'm in no mood for a purificatory bath and a change of clothes. But I'll deal with you first thing tomorrow morning. Just you wait.'

'You've already done that so many times in the past!' Dharama shot back contemptuously, as he walked off. 'What's new about that threat of yours?'

'You saw it, Chhakadi, my boy, didn't you?' Hari Mishra huffed. 'Who is it that's emboldened these low-caste creatures? None other than your brother, your precious brother, Baraju! A man like Dharama, who'd stammer when he had to utter his father's name, has become so bold as to fling words in my face, and get away with it too! Do you know what treatment people like him deserve? A sound thrashing! A thrashing when they sit down, a thrashing when they stand up. That's the only way to straighten out their kind. But what does Baraju Pradhan do? He hobnobs with them. Teaches them wrong things. Can't then blame the low-castes if they get notions. Remember the lawsuit I filed against Ghana Khatei. Your big brother went round criticizing me so much that I couldn't scrounge up a witness. Seems the whole wide world is only full of liars and crooks, and Baraju's the only shining creature of truth. You tell me, Chhakadi, is there a single soul in the entire creation who's never told a lie in his life?'

'But, Uncle,' said Chhakadi, 'that's what people swear: that my brother hasn't told a single lie since he was born!'

'Boy, he might be able to throw dust in the eyes of fools and dimwits, but can he dupe people like you and me? You live with him under the same roof, so you must have already noticed that Baraju and his wife don't speak the same tongue!'

'Haven't I, Uncle! I don't need someone like this untouchable Dharama to make me see things. The fellow had the cheek to tell me I'm already in dire straits where the shop's concerned.'

'I'd have slapped him until his cheeks turned red if I weren't in my good clothes. He should thank his lucky stars.'

Dharama's words had been downright insulting, and Chhakadi would have been mighty pleased if the fellow's face had turned red, or black or whatever. He seized upon Hari Mishra's assurance. 'But come tomorrow morning, you must show him his place, Uncle.' He began to feel instantly better as he imagined the beating the untouchable would receive the next morning.

'Oh, you don't have to tell me that, son,' Hari Mishra assured him. 'Tell you what, why don't you come along to my place tomorrow morning to witness the show? What Dharama badly needs this time is more than the usual treatment. This time I'll tie him up with the ropes for tethering cattle. I'll pin him to a coconut tree and lash him with poison ivy. My dear boy, fellows like Dharama can be fixed within an hour, but what about that brother of yours? We might be able to shut Dharama up, but what shall we do when a whole lot of people encouraged by your brother jump into the fray? How do we fight a mob? How could Baraju go and goad a rank outsider like that untouchable into raising his voice against his own younger brother, someone he still lives with under the same roof? Does that untouchable Dharama even count as a man? Someone who's illiterate into the bargain! How could Dharama have come to understand you've run through the whole investment and are now in a bad situation? Somebody must have planted the idea in his mind. I can't think of anyone other than Baraju. Who else? Don't tell me I'm losing my marbles.'

'I've caught on, Uncle, I have. I may have put off my wife for a long time, I might not have heeded her words until now, but sometimes she does come out with very accurate observations. Not a bit of untruth in those words of hers. She's been after me for a family partition. Your brother, she says, has three daughters to marry off. Where's the money for the weddings going to come from if not the common income of the household? Surely not from nowhere! Why must we put up with all that nonsense, what sins have we committed, why should we work ourselves to death just to see strangers do well at our expense?'

Strangers! Chhakadi felt a twinge of regret as soon as the word had escaped his lips, but he clamped down on his feelings. Of course his brother and his family had become strangers. What else, if not strangers? They had already started behaving like that. His sister-in-law was making her purchases of betel leaves and nuts from somewhere else, not from his shop. And between them, the two women went for days without exchanging a word; catching them chatting with each other could happen only in a dream. Whenever they did exchange a few words, they fought. Even the brothers were no longer of the same mind, and they too had grown apart. Did his brother ever take the trouble to explain how everything worked to him? If they had fallen mentally apart, why pay lip-service to living together?

Mishra saw an opening. 'You mentioned your wife, Chhakadi, didn't you? Remember, a wife's the goddess of the home. We men, what do we ever do? How little we do to look after our home! Men only do the chores outside, but indoors women have always taken care of everything. Illiterate fools like Dharama Das might call someone who defers to his wife henpecked, but what does the opinion of a non-entity like him matter? My own lady, my son Basua's mother, didn't she go after me insisting on a family partition from day one? But did I pay her any heed for a long time? Why not? Because the advice was coming from a woman! Stupid, stupid me. And when I did finally force a family partition, did any calamity befall me? Am I now running around in places like Calcutta or Midnapore, as do your elder brother and my younger brother Kela, looking for employment as cooks or simply passing the bowl around begging?'

'Reduced to begging, you? Uncle, don't even utter such things. Who in this village would let you come to such a sorry pass? Don't ever say such things!'

'Heh, heh! You're too simple, too innocent, my boy. I'm not suggesting you'll be reduced to begging someday. Why, you own ten acres of farmland, prime paddy fields, several head of cattle; you come from ancient stock too. Your family has been well known for the last seven generations. But, Chhakadi my boy, no matter what you may say, I'd put down the present state of your affairs to your own stupidity and inefficiency.'

'But, Uncle, you know quite well that somebody in the family doesn't want me to master the art of farming.'

Mishra snorted derisively. 'But who's he to keep you from learning the ropes? Besides, you aren't a child any more, not still being breastfed are you?'

'Right, Uncle. Beginning this year, I'm going to do what Chandra Siyal has suggested: claim half the green-gram harvest. And half the paddy crop too. I'm going to pile my share in a different heap; I'm going to have my own corner of the barnyard from now on. When I asked Chandra to tell me how to go about it, since I knew very well the entire labour on the fields and farms had been my brother's, he said: "How does one din some sense into that thick skull of yours? What do you mean it's entirely your brother's labour? Don't you rightfully own half the land? Didn't your brother spend money out of the family funds to engage us farmhands? Your brother might have personally pitched in a little when it came to the actual work in the fields, kneeling down beside us farmhands to pull out weeds or steer the ploughshare for a while, but that doesn't mean he shouldn't share the harvest with you. All the sharecroppers you see around, don't they share in the harvest with the landowners?" Chandra might come from a low caste, Uncle, but he has a lot of sense in that little head of his for sure. When I told my wife what he'd said, she couldn't stop crowing: "Don't even angle for a second opinion from me. Go spruce up the corner of the barnyard where we'll store our half of the harvest."'

'God, how long has it taken me to hear such decisive words from you,' Hari Mishra said. 'This is the right decision. It can't be considered an insult. And it doesn't mean you're going to divide the pots and pans or cook separately. For the last ten years it was the elder brother looking after everything; from now on the younger has come of age and will look after his own interests. Well, that's an arrangement nobody can find fault with. Nobody can blame the younger brother. And it's totally correct too. You mentioned Chandra Siyal, didn't you? He's someone who could squeeze water out of a dry log, that man. Would I have made him my factotum if I didn't know his worth?'

God alone knew where Chandra Siyal had been hiding, but he materialized just then with his long and stout bamboo staff. He leaned it against the doorway of Chhakadi's shop and bowed low to Hari Mishra.

'You'll live to be a hundred,' said Hari Mishra, 'appearing just when we were talking of you. What's new?'

Chandra was his most trusted factotum. He collected all sorts of news from around—who sneezed, who smiled, who didn't like this or that, who was saying what—and relayed it to his master. Just as devotees seeking the blessings of Lord Shiva first caress the image of His mount the holy bull or embrace the image of Garuda when they come to worship Lord Vishnu in His temple, people wishing to get into Hari Mishra's good books first cultivated Chandra. According to Baraju, what was true of Shiva's bull or Vishnu's Garuda or Hari Mishra's Chandra Siyal was also true of kings, emperors and chieftains. Their underlings—clerks, bureaucrats, surveyors, peons, messengers—had to be appeased first.

Chandra Siyal gave a devious grin. 'Big news, master. But I can convey it in strict privacy only.'

'Hang privacy. Chhakadi here is like my own son. So don't be wary of him, he won't breathe a word to anyone.'

'Sir, you know Sadei Barik. His son-in-law has been away in Calcutta for the last two years, so his daughter's been living with him. You must have heard about what happened with her last year . . . but the evidence was suppressed so well, nobody was any the wiser . . . but this year it's different . . . go to his banana grove and you'll find a newborn babe bawling at the top of his lungs.'

'What, the child's still alive?'

'And bawling to bring the roof down, sir. The banana grove's ringing with the baby's crying. And the woman who gave birth to it is now back in her kitchen, washed clean of her sins! It's Saradi Bou who wised me up to this just a short while ago. But for her I wouldn't have gotten wind of it.'

'Another case of adultery? Of rape possibly?' Hari Mishra was spluttering. 'And the child's still alive and kicking! Things would have been a bit better if it were dead. Never mind. Go tell the chowkidar to rush to the police station to file the information. Any idea what Sadei Barik's up to at the moment?'

'Precious little he can do now, sir. The news is already all over the village. But he might still try to brazen it out. You know he won't admit easily.'

'Never mind. No matter whatever he's up to now, he'll come to me in the end. As the saying goes, the parboiled paddy is destined to come to the husking paddle. Go tell the chowkidar.' He turned to Chhakadi. 'You see my sorry plight, my boy. I don't have a minute of rest to myself; I won't even be able to give up the ghost in peace. Go on, son, shut the shop and head home. And remember, don't ever hesitate to bring things to my notice or ask for my advice whenever necessary.'

'You won't have to remind me a second time, Uncle.'

*

There were enough banana groves and jute fields in every village around. A newborn's cries could be made out from anywhere—from underneath the screw-pine bushes or on the banks of a pond. What miseries people bring upon themselves! Who could help them? Hari Mishra's fortune grew, people like Sadei Barik came to utter ruin, Baraju Pradhan's eyes welled up with tears whenever he heard an abandoned infant's cries. But what could even the most powerful and devious on earth do to someone whom the gods had decided to love and protect?

8

Hara Bou, Hara's mother, made all manner of pledges and promises to the gods and goddesses: 'Mother Mangala, I'll give you a ritual bath if my husband returns safe and sound . . . Lord Kapileswar, I'll offer you 100,000 gayasa flowers, to make sure my man gets back home soon unharmed . . .'

Nobody had any clue where Baraju spent those five days away from home. But on the evening of the day Saradi Bou persuaded Hara Bou to obtain the water with magical powers he showed up.

In the evening, as Hara Bou sat rolling wicks to light at the tulsi platform, Moti rushed in from outdoors, screaming, 'Mother, father's back!' The heady feelings that swirled around in Hara Bou's mind—only she experienced what they were.

When Baraju stopped in the middle of the courtyard and his daughter Suna fetched him a jug of water to wash his feet, Hara Bou raised her head and looked him over. His face was drawn and darker; his belly had shrunk, almost touching his back; his hair, without oil for days was dry and unkempt and danced in the breeze. She laid her wick-

rolling aside and, breaking down like a child, rushed into their room in tears.

Baraju was back home, but he continued to wallow in misery. The expression on his face remained as heavy and grim as before. He neither ate heartily nor took an interest in anything. No matter how many times his wife asked him about some thing, he answered in monosyllables and without mirth or warmth.

Netramani, who had grown used to her sari slipping off her head—she no longer bothered to observe the required decorum and etiquette in the presence of elders—was all smiles. She grinned at her husband Chhakadi, curling her red, betel-juice-stained lips. 'Are you watching the show the woman's putting up? Will there be an end to it? Every bit of it's just for us!'

'Of course!' Chhakadi was delighted to see smiles back on his wife's face. 'All for show!'

'But have you understood what's behind it?' she asked. 'The weddings of Suna and Moti aren't far off. But then you—you get taken in by anything. I know with what gusto you'll dive into the celebrations—you'll sing, you'll dance. A lot. But I'm telling you right now—I'm not going to hang around here during the weddings. You'll have to take me back to my parents. I'll stay with them until the damn celebrations have come to an end.'

Chhakadi's wits deserted him at once. He knew that if she visited her parents, she would be gone for a year or maybe longer. Her mother would start moaning and sighing over how much weight her darling daughter had lost and use every trick in the book to prolong her stay another couple of months. Her father would keep saying, what's the rush, why does the poor dear have to hurry back to her in-laws, are ants carrying away the jaggery from the pots over there? 'Don't get ahead of yourself, woman,' he said. 'Do you think the family's still going to be together then?'

*

Hara Bou's back was broken. Everyone in the village was saying Baraju left home because he couldn't get along with his wife. Already the younger sister-in-law and her husband were full of sly smiles at her wretched plight. Why had all this been written in her fate? She was so filled with shame and contrition she was reluctant to face her neighbours. Whoever she ran into seemed to break into a crooked smile and confront her: 'So, Hara Bou, was it a fight between you and your husband that drove him from home?'

But why mind their titters, she thought. She wouldn't pay them any attention, especially when she could do nothing about them. Nothing would matter if only her husband was happy and cheerful again, ate heartily, spoke pleasantly. What did that widow Saradi Bou do with the money she had taken to get things back on an even keel? Nothing seemed to have worked yet.

She tried her best to engage Baraju in conversation, telling him about the daughters' wedding dates and about the kind of in-laws she would prefer. But he wasn't forthcoming; he refused to speak his mind and was evasive.

'You've become so distant,' she complained. 'You keep yourself to yourself. Who's going to look around for matches for the girls—me?'

'Did I say you'd have to?'

'Or do you want the girls to remain unmarried? Between brothers there're bound to be splits and divisions. Chhakadi might insist on a family partition tomorrow—already plans are afoot.'

'Hara Bou,' he said quietly, 'did I ask you to fill me in on what's happening at home?'

Her face fell. But if she didn't say anything he would simply ignore her. 'Have you left me with even a shred of self-respect? And you're still being sarcastic? At the slightest provocation you took off God knows where and went without food and water for days. Tell me when have I been disobedient or acted wilfully or not deferred to you!' She felt hot tears sting her eyes.

'I'm not asking you to obey me or to defer to me. You'll have to think and figure out for yourself what will make this household run smoothly. You've got to look for the answers.'

'Oh, I'm a mere woman. What do the tribe of women know of the complex ways of the world? Why don't you tell me what will work, what will work well enough?'

It didn't escape Baraju that his wife had softened a bit. Maybe she could now be convinced to behave in a proper manner. 'Good,' he said. 'Here's how you can go about it: Never pick a fight, and keep your mouth shut tight even when the younger sister-in-law spoils for one. Don't get your dander up even when she criticizes you or me or takes it out on the children. Can't you, who're used to observing so many fasts and vigils round the year, add this to your repertoire? Tell me, are you capable of this or not?'

'Why not?'

Baraju sensed she lacked conviction. And he wasn't wrong either, because soon afterwards she became involved in a blazing row with the younger woman. But she did bite her tongue the moment she remembered her promise. How could she have forgotten it so quickly, no matter how angry she was?

'Oh, how well you kept your promise!' said Baraju, taking a dig at her.

She sulked, her nostrils quivering. 'Away with you! I didn't remember in time. Oh, this pitiful fire-singed mind of mine!'

'Never mind this time. But if you forget again, I'll be free to do as I please.'

She panicked. Who knew what he would get up to? But how long could she stand the younger sister-in-law taking it out on her children in her presence? How would she swallow all that in silence? What nonsense was her husband asking her to put up with?

It dawned on Baraju that his wife would never turn over a new leaf, even if he kept away from home. He would have to be around, at home, to reach his goal. If she went back on her pledge, he would enforce his—observe total silence, stop talking altogether, not just to her but to everyone, with no exceptions. Not talking only to her wouldn't help, since she could always keep a line of communication open through the children.

*

Eight or ten days passed. Although her blood was boiling, Hara Bou kept her mouth shut, putting up with every provocation Netramani threw at her. The younger woman could scream and shout all she wanted, call her names and say horrible things to her—'childless widow', 'son-eater', 'daughter's husband's killer', 'may she burn in hell', 'may she catch fire and be reduced to ashes', and so on and so forth—until she was spent. Hara Bou would put up with it all in silence. She might respond just a tiny bit, just a little, and in the lowest of voices, if Baraju was away, before relapsing into silence again. She knew the younger woman would raise her voice if she overheard a word she whispered. And it would reach Baraju's ears if he were to come back home unexpectedly. As long as he was in or around home, she would keep her lips hermetically sealed, she vowed.

On that particular day, Baraju returned home sooner than usual from the field with the team of oxen. Before he had unyoked the animals and tethered them in the cow shed, the shouts and screams from inside the house hit him. His wife seemed to put in a sentence or two here and there, now and then, like feeding pieces of straw to the raging fire of the younger daughter-in-law. Netramani was in full cry.

His wife stopped short at the sight of him, biting her tongue. One look at his face and she was petrified. But

Netramani, beyond all sense of decorum and politeness, didn't stop, although her voice did drop a decibel.

Baraju thought he must truly be the most miserable sinner on the face of the earth. His household was falling apart because of him. He had lost his prestige, his standing in the community, in the village; the reputation of his family was in tatters. What next—a family partition, a wall up the middle of the courtyard? But would even that put an end to the squabbles and fights? Everything would still remain a bone of contention—who dug a hole in the ground, even if it was in his part of the courtyard, who threw the kitchen ashes where, whose cat crossed over to the other side; the seeds of quarrel lay buried in every day-to-day activity. Family partition didn't mean they would move elsewhere and separate geographically; the brothers would inhabit the same space as before. Each would continue to fight the demons of his mind, no matter where he lived—in the same neighbourhood, in the same village, in the same society! Wouldn't it make more sense to go and live in the depths of the forest?

Baraju put into motion the plan he had decided on: he sank into silence. He maintained it strictly, not uttering a word no matter how insistently his children and wife plied him with questions. This drove Hara Bou into a panic: What new nonsense was this? Sure he could get by without uttering a word, but what kind of a life would that be? For once she didn't know whether to laugh or cry.

The days dragged on.

Baraju refused to speak, simply looking on, sometimes just staring vacantly.

In the past, he wouldn't sit down to a meal unless there was fish or meat, and Hara Bou had had to find some—a pair of tiny fried or dried fish—and roast them wrapped in leaves. These days, though, he resolutely stayed away from the dishes he loved. He had taken a pledge and wasn't going to break it anytime soon, not until his wishes had been realized. He gave up using oil—his dry hair twirled about in the breeze, his skin became rough and ashen. Whenever his wife came to massage his tired old feet with oil at bedtime, he would get up and leave in a huff. In the beginning, when it all began, his wife was amused and simply smiled, but of late she just wanted to hang her head and bitterly cry her heart out.

On the evening of the new moon festival of Shravana, when coconut rice cakes are prepared, Hara Bou remembered how fond Baraju was of these. She added an extra portion of grated coconut to the soaked rice, grinding them into an extremely smooth paste to bake fluffy cakes. She wanted her husband to eat his fill of them.

Baraju sat in the doorway twisting wild grass into rope for a new mat, his two children beside him. Hara Bou swept the place clean with a broom and set a platter of cakes in front of him. By the time she could bring a bowl of milk, a plate of stewed vegetables and a ball of jaggery, Baraju had got up, after eating only half a cake.

That was just too much for her, and Hara Bou broke into convulsive sobs. 'Why're you punishing me? I beg you to eat some more cakes. I'll do anything you ask of me, I swear. I swear by God.'

Baraju was aware his wife had stopped bickering with Netramani ever since he had started observing his silence. But that wasn't enough. There were higher peaks to scale. The poison was in her mind, in her heart. Until that was removed there was still work to do.

But he spoke.

Hara Bou was thrilled.

'So you want me to speak again?' Baraju said. 'Then will you do what I ask?'

'Absolutely. I'll obey your every command.'

'No, why not think for yourself and see where your best qualities lie?'

'No, I don't know anything. I can't think things through. Spell things out for me and I'll act as you want.'

'Exactly as I say?'

'Exactly as you say!' Tears streamed down her cheeks.

Chhakadi and Netramani stole into the courtyard a couple of times just to enjoy the unfolding spectacle. Baraju, his hair moving in the breeze, resembled a ghost, and his once proud, unbending wife, finally broken, her head bowed, was grasping her husband's hands. The apparent theatricality of it drove them back into their bedroom, where they were overcome with such wild fits of helpless laughter they had to gag themselves.

Baraju stood his ground like an unmoved stone. 'Promise me that on your own you'll never ever start a shouting match, let alone pick a fight, with the younger daughter-in-law, that you'll never vie with her for anything.'

Hara Bou's tears fell thick and fast and ran right down to her feet. Still in the grip of convulsive sobs, she promised, 'Never will I engage in a row with her, never will I pick a fight with her.'

'Will you hold your tongue no matter what the provocation?'

'I promise to hold my tongue no matter what the provocation.'

'Come, let's go into our room. I'll tell you the rest you must do.'

A few fat drops of her tears fell on his feet. Did they scald his stony feet?

Hara Bou sensed her enemies were laughing at her. But what did that matter now? She had been reduced to a laughing stock by none other than her own husband. And he had reduced himself to a laughing stock too. Robbed of her self-respect, there now wasn't anybody or anything that could mortify her any more. Certainly not Chhakadi or his wife, or the neighbours. She hung on to her husband's arm and stopped him. 'Spit it out here, whatever you have in mind. Here. Now. There's nothing to hide.'

Baraju seemed to have taken leave of his sense of shame. He had no idea how deeply he had already humiliated his wife, the amount of pain he had inflicted on her—the woman who was not only his wife but the mother of their children too, she who represented womanhood worshipped as Lakshmi, Shakti, Devi, Durga. How could he have rejected her? On the other hand, he was brimming over with joy that for once his wife wasn't being arrogant and unyielding.

'Promise me that a goodly share of whatever's cooked at home, beginning with dishes with ghee and milk, will be served first to Chhakadi and his wife, that you'll personally see to their meals before anyone else's. You'll think of your children only afterwards. And you and I will have our meals last, only at the end.'

Hara Bou shut her eyes as she repeated after him like a parrot: children's meals after Chhakadi and Netramani's, hers and her husband's at the end. After all the children, they didn't belong to her alone—if he was fine with them eating after his brother had, so be it. All she had to do was harden herself into a stone.

With a wan smile, Baraju cautioned her: 'Look, you've agreed to all my conditions with your hand on mine. If you don't follow them, I'll take it you no longer care for me.'

Hara Bou nearly died of shame. How long had she been holding her husband's hand?

Baraju sat down to the plate of the fluffy coconut rice cakes. He spoke pleasantly to the children. Although her pride had taken a severe beating, Hara Bou melted when she heard him ask for an extra helping of this or that—a chilli, some stewed vegetables—and the courtyard became too small for her strides. A heavy weight had been taken off her chest; she felt light. The stone images of the gods seemed to have come alive—both home and outside seemed bathed in peace and brightness.

'Go ask Chhakadi to come and join me,' Baraju said.

She forgot that this was the same Chhakadi who had lunged to hit her in the past, not once but three times. She walked to her brother-in-law's room as if in a trance.

But Chhakadi stalked off angrily, saying he was late for his shop.

For once Hara Bou didn't take offence. She was suddenly so full of exhilaration she found not only him but everyone else pleasant; she was filled with a desire to chat with everyone. She wouldn't tell Baraju that Chhakadi had walked off in a huff. She approached the younger daughter-in-law: 'Junior, come and have a few cakes with me. No point in waiting for Chhakadi. Once he walks out, God alone knows when he'll be back.'

The younger woman took this badly, thinking her elder sister-in-law was now showing off because she had made up with her husband. 'No way,' she said with a scowl. 'I can't be bothered to eat now. I'll eat afterwards.'

Hara Bou laughed. 'Sister, forget the past. I might have said many unpleasant things to you in the past, but don't hold any of that against me. You must forgive me.'

Hara Bou's words pricked Netramani like needles. What a brazen display she was making! Just because she had once again found favour with her husband. Until now they had been so bitterly at odds that if the husband faced one way the wife looked in the opposite direction. 'No, I don't hold a grudge against anyone. Why should anyone be unpleasant to me, or I to anyone?'

Hara Bou didn't know what else to say. She went back and reported to Baraju all that had transpired.

He took everything in silence. 'Then please go without food until the younger daughter-in-law has had hers.'

She looked up at him, beaming brightly. And he warmly smiled back.

Neither could recall when they had last exchanged such sweet smiles. Their happiness seemed mirrored in each other's face. Like the reflection of the full moon of Kumara Purnima on a sheet of clean blue water at the end of the month of Ashwina, the moon wondering if it had fallen in the water and the water if it were inside the moon. Both in shivers, both in goose bumps.

The radiant smile on his wife's face produced in Baraju a sense of joy he hadn't known before. It made him realize that since his wedding day he had merely got along with his wife without any great sense of togetherness, that there had always been a wall between them. Though tied together through the knot of matrimony, they were ever apart, too far from each other mentally. That wall had now crumbled and husband and wife had become closer than ever before. At the touch of the philosopher's stone within Baraju's heart, the iron in Hara Bou's soul had turned to gold. Both had awakened. He was as surprised at her transformation as she was at his. She marvelled at the new being she had metamorphosed into. Every human heart possesses within it a philosopher's stone, which can turn any base metal into gold.

Chhakadi returned home at midnight. Neither his wife nor his sister-in-law had eaten, waiting for him to have his meal first. This didn't matter much to the older woman; she was feeling bad only on account of the younger. How rude the younger woman had been to her children! And so full of ill will towards Baraju too. And tonight it was for her sake that she, Hara Bou, was keeping a fast!

'Boy,' Baraju accosted his younger brother as soon as he reached home. 'Where were you until midnight?' He called out to his wife. 'Hurry up and give him something to eat. He must be starving.' At dinner every night in the past he had looked for his younger brother. Some days the boy hadn't returned home, some days he had already had his food and gone to bed.

Chhakadi avoided speaking with his brother face to face, let alone start arguments with him. All his conversations were with his wife Netramani, just as all his fights were with his sister-in-law. But all of that took place behind his elder brother's back. He might sit and conspire with Hari Mishra for hours on end, but whenever he ran into Baraju he couldn't hurry away fast enough. No matter how sharply his wife twisted his tail, he could never muster the courage to confront Baraju. Oh, the shame of it.

He was whispering with his wife in his bedroom when Baraju called out to him once again. 'Where're you stuck, boy? The food's getting cold.'

'Coming,' said Chhakadi, hurrying to wash his feet before sitting down to his meal.

Hara Bou went to Netramani again. 'Sister, come, let's eat now. All the others have had theirs and are already in bed. What crimes have you and I committed that we must go without a bite for any longer?'

'But why the hell are you waiting for me?' the younger woman retorted in irritation. Why was love being showered on her tonight? Why was Hara Bou fawning and fussing over her, as if the cakes wouldn't go down her gullet if she, Netramani, chose to fast?

Hara Bou entered her room in a state of euphoria she hadn't known since her marriage twenty years earlier. For once, she felt she had not a single enemy or adversary in the whole wide world; everyone seemed so dear and precious. True, she was twenty years older and her looks had faded, but how beautiful she felt tonight. That beauty wouldn't fade, not in five years or ten—it would remain forever, deathless. 'Listen,' she told her husband. 'Netramani didn't care for the sari you bought her for Hara's wedding. This time for Suna's wedding you must buy a very good one.'

Baraju couldn't believe his ears. Was it really Hara Bou who was pitching for a good sari for Chhakadi's wife? Was this the same woman whose belly button jumped when Netramani got something nice? 'Definitely!' teased Baraju. 'But what about you?'

'Am I so young that I'd hanker after a good sari? It's all right with me if the younger ones wear the nice saris.'

'Really? Are you telling the truth?'

'My, why do you think you alone tell the truth? Is everyone else a liar?'

'Not at all, I didn't say that. It's hard to believe you're the same person! I hope your heart remains as pure as it is now.'

Hara Bou laughed. 'Have no fear, it will. Why, what do you imagine it'll change into?'

'Promise me your heart will remain as pure even if we're forced to go begging from door to door.'

'Why are you having such fears? Are you afraid I'll act like an uppity little rich lady if you become a beggar? Forget it. My heart will remain true even if it costs me my life.'

Baraju was thrilled: the god within her had vanquished her demons.

The next morning when Hara Bou went to the pond for her bath, she was still feeling the shivers of unalloyed joy, as if she had suddenly found the husband she had lost over a century ago. When Saradi Bou and Widow Panda joined her, not a word of condemnation of her brother-in-law and his wife escaped her lips. 'What do we have to worry about, after all? Once we marry off the two girls, there'll be nothing more to worry about. Then it's all Chhakadi and his wife's to enjoy— the land, the farms, the homestead, everything. As the saying goes, if you want to live in a family you must put up with little pinpricks, sometimes even with falling rocks. So why should I continue to nurse a grudge? A grudge against whom—my own brother-in-law and his wife? Whatever for? In this world, nobody's running away with anything when they die. Nobody carries anything off from here to the hereafter.'

The two women were taken by surprise to hear such lofty words from Hara Bou's lips.

And Hara Bou was unstoppable. 'My husband, he explained that it takes two hands to clap, that one hand doesn't the sound of clapping make. So I can't claim to be entirely above reproach and place the blame squarely on them. After all, they're younger than I am. Whose fault is it if an older, more experienced person finds fault with the words of the callow and the young? I've given this a lot of thought. Frankly, I'm not without blame. Never mind that Netramani doesn't lift her little finger to help with the chores around the house, what have *I* ever done for her? How well my husband explained it. All human beings, he says, tend to make light of their own faults while making a mountain of a molehill when it comes to those of others. How true! All my life I have never blamed myself for anything, not once. As if I were a saint, a paragon of virtue.' She stopped, realizing she had gone on and on in praise of her husband. 'Sisters,' she said, changing her sari, 'why don't you come home with me? I could give you some ground gram and curried spinach.'

The two women fell from the skies. Since when had Hara Bou become so generous?

Hara Bou fulfilled the promises she had made, down to the smallest letter. She looked after her brother-in-law and his wife very well; they came ahead of everyone else, including her children.

*

Netramani was unfazed; she took it all in her stride. She felt she deserved all the concern and consideration the older woman was showing. If she hadn't been pampered until now, that was the older woman's fault; she was the one to blame. If she ever did an extra bit of housework she thought she was doing Hara Bou a favour. After all, six of the family of eight were Hara Bou's. So rightfully three quarters of all household chores should fall to the older woman. Why should Netramani volunteer to attend to them?

9

'Oh Dharama,' Baraju cried out, as he made his way into the poor fellow's hut. 'Who flogged you so viciously?'

The sight of Dharama brought tears to his eyes. The poor fellow's body was an ugly mess of welts and bruises. He had been beaten within an inch of his life, both with branches of poison ivy and a stick. Dhani Bou, his wife, sat beside him, massaging him with linseed oil.

'Who did this?'

'Haven't you heard, Baraju Bhai?' Dharama croaked between groans. 'Weren't you home?' He turned to his wife. 'Woman, go get a slat of wood for Baraju Bhai to sit on.' Then turning to Baraju, 'It was that devil of a servant boy—that Chandra Siyal—at the command of his master, the Brahmin.'

'Why, whatever on earth for?'

'Poor me! Then you don't know a thing, do you? That Brahmin Hari Mishra, he took it out on me. He was nursing a grudge against me for standing up to him a bit at your brother Chhakadi's shop. Pretty annoyed, I'd say, since then. And this morning he got the opportunity

107

he was looking for when the cattle I was herding strayed into his banana grove. He caught and tied some of them to a coconut tree. What could I tell him, what could I say to calm him down? You know me, I've never been a smooth-talker.'

Tears rolled down Baraju's cheeks. 'Ah, my poor Dharama!'

The world was full of poor Dharamas—all of them getting beaten, their bodies riddled with welts. But then there was no dearth of Barajus either, and all dripping with the milk of human kindness, tears and sympathy. But nothing changed. What difference did they make? None!

'Never mind,' Dharama sighed. 'This time they got me. Someday I'll have my chance. I'll be sure to settle the score with that Mishra and his boy. Little do I care for my life. I live by my labour, I've nothing to lose. No land, no property to worry about. Mishra's been telling me that my homestead too has been recorded in his name in the last land-settlement records, that he'll grow aubergines on it once he boots me out. But why should he take the trouble, I'll make it easier for him by moving out on my own. I've been telling Dhani Bou to forget me, to go smash her bangles and become a widow. In our Bauri caste, it's easy to marry again and move in with another man. As long as you live by the sweat of your brow, you won't be without a morsel of food wherever you go. As long as you're able to work with your hands and legs, you won't starve to death!'

Baraju didn't understand. 'Now you're raving like a madman.'

'Am I, brother?' Dharama pointed to a razor-sharp knife. 'I've bathed it with *punnag* oil and anointed it with vermilion. Take a good look at it. Isn't it sharp enough to slice a man's head off?'

A shudder ran down Baraju's spine and he leaned back. 'What're you babbling on about?'

Dharama rolled his eyes. 'What am I jabbering about, huh? I'll tell you, I'll tell the whole wide world. Whether I die now or later, I'm no longer afraid of anyone. To me, death by hanging is no different than passing away in my bed at home. Dharama's no longer scared of death.'

Baraju was shaking like a palm leaf in the breeze. What was all this Dharama was going on about? 'Dharama, my brother,' he begged, grasping his hands. 'Calm down, calm down. I came to ask you over to Goddess Mangala's temple for the evening service. Will you be able to make it?'

For Dharama, the evening service of the goddess wasn't important at all. 'Listen, Baraju Bhai. No matter in which direction the dead man's head rolls, east or west, Dharama Bauri will soon smear the blood of Hari Mishra across his forehead.'

'Dharama, my brother,' Baraju begged again. 'Calm down. Listen to me. Don't let your senses take leave of you. Promise me you'll join me for the evening service. Will you be able to make it?'

'Not able to make it? Why, what's wrong with me? I've had worse hidings before, this is nothing.'

That evening, Dharama limped to the temple of Goddess Mangala. Baraju was already there. Before long others arrived in ones and twos—Jui Khatei, Uda Sutar, Rup Jena, Jadu Dalei and several others. After bowing to the goddess, they all sat under the bower of *malati* flowers.

'Baraju Bhai,' Jadu Dalei began. 'Blame it on fate. How else can you explain why a poor man like Dharama, who does no one any harm, was beaten up so badly?'

'But I explained that to you the other day,' Baraju said. 'It's Hari Mishra who decides Dharama's fate. He's the one who makes and undoes Dharama's life. For good or for bad, he controls what happens to this poor man, through his whims and caprices.'

'Brother, I don't buy that Hari Mishra's has control over Dharama's destiny. It's Dharama's destiny that controls Hari Mishra's.'

'One and the same thing, no matter how you put it. Ravana was as much Ram's destiny as Ram was Ravana's. But you can't simply put the blame on karma alone, and then close your eyes and slide into deep meditation! There are so many things people can use to fend off bad karma, to ward off the evil glance of hostile stars.'

'I agree with you, brother,' said someone.

'So what do we do now to ward off the bad stars staring down at us?'

From the back of the crowd, Dharama piped up. 'Baraju Bhai, remember what I told you earlier in the day.'

Baraju winced. 'Today it was Hari Mishra, tomorrow it'll be the zamindar's accountant, the next day the moneylender's debt collector. Have we been born only to be roughed up by such elements? Is that our destiny, eh?'

'Surely not,' shouted someone. 'We must give as good as we get! Get roughed up, go rough up. Equally!'

'That's just bravado, brother! See, we're so many farming families here in this village, but has any one of us ever plucked up the courage to take revenge against anyone who oppresses us? No, it's our destiny to lie low. Not that we don't ever put people down; we do. But they're always our own, our family members, our relations. And why? Because we can't sort out our quarrels and feuds and problems amongst ourselves. We always look for outside intervention, we need judges from the outside.'

'Never uttered a truer thing, brother,' said Uda Sutar. 'How can land surveyors make money off us unless we fight amongst ourselves? We all know which pieces of land have been in our families for seven generations. What does it matter if the land surveyors or registrars record them under somebody else's name in the official documents? If we stick to cultivating the land that belongs to us regardless of whose name's on the official documents, surely no one can force us to grab hold of somebody else's land?'

'Today it was Dharama who was flogged. And who did it? If there weren't people like Chandra Siyal amongst us, Hari Mishra couldn't have beaten and terrorized so many people. The sad fact's we lack unity. When Dharama's flogged, his neighbour Uda gloats: good, good, that Dharama had it coming to him! But if we all felt the sting of the lashes when Dharama was being flogged, if we all took it as our loss when Dharama's house went up in flames, if we all felt Apartia's sickness as something happening in our family, if everyone tried to lessen the losses others suffer, helped overcome sickness and other tragedies and came to their rescue, then all our sorrows would melt and flow away like water in the river. Could Hari Mishra, all by himself, continue to behave so badly when he's surrounded by so many good men? Many a man stood and watched when Dharama was flogged. Did even one lift his little finger to stop it?'

'What could we have done?' two or three voices lifted up. 'Pitch in and get beaten ourselves?'

'Yes,' Baraju shot back. 'Yes, get beaten good and proper. Weren't you whipped when poor Dharama was? One of you was the victim of a thrashing today, tomorrow it'll be someone else. So how do you see it—was it Dharama alone who was beaten, or all of you?'

'All of us of course,' said old Ratana Bhoi. 'That's the right way to look at it.'

'But what else could have been done?' Rup Jena persisted. 'You know Hari Mishra. Would he have listened to anyone, he who's used to crushing the raised hood of an enraged cobra?'

'But suppose ten of you had rushed to surround Dharama and said politely to Hari Mishra, "Sir, to err is human, it's Dharama today, it'll be someone else tomorrow, but you're a big shot, herding men as we do cattle, so please listen to us, take our entreaties kindly. We're begging you to let Dharama's fault be examined and decided by the five elders. Punish him by all means if he's found guilty, but if you don't listen to us and beat Dharama, you might as well start by beating us all."'

Rup Jena scoffed. 'And would Hari Mishra have paid any heed? The only outcome would have been that we too would have been thrashed black and blue.'

Baraju flared up. 'And wouldn't that have been just wonderful! You being beaten in lieu of your brother Dharama—what's wrong with that? Nothing. Today Hari Mishra thrashed Dharama, tomorrow he'll do the same to you, and it'll be my turn the day after. How many people can he thrash, how long can he go on? He has been at this for a long time and all we've done is hide at home. What if we all join together and face him? Wouldn't that be heroic, wouldn't that be showing a little bit of spine?'

'Have virtue and goodness vanished from the face of the earth?' Jadu Dalei wailed. 'Has vice totally taken over?'

'Stop all this high-sounding talk,' Rup sneered. 'There're so many of us assembled here, but is anyone prepared to take him on?'

'I am!' Baraju jumped to his feet. 'I'm prepared to go and fall at Hari Mishra's feet and plead with him. If he brushes me aside, I'll go hug Dharama and dare Mishra, "Sir, flog me first, as much as you can; I'm Dharama's brother and willing to be beaten in his place." And I won't let go of Dharama even if he kills me. It's better to die than to put up with pointless, meaningless beatings. What difference does it make? So what if the entire population of the village is wiped out, or one hundred families of the Pradhan colony disappear? If it pleases Hari Mishra to kill everyone around and be the lone survivor, if he wants to take all of our homesteads to expand his own, then may he live alone and may he prosper. If we don't matter, we're better off dead than existing as insects or worms! But tell me, do you people really feel we're so helpless, so hopeless? Remember, the same *duba* grass which sheep and goats trample underfoot makes the twine used to tie up and secure animals like elephants. Will it ever come to pass that a hundred families will perish and Mishra alone will live on in this village?'

'No, no,' someone shouted. 'Unthinkable. Unbelievable.'

'It's our own fault we're miserable. If we join hands, the tribe of Hari Mishra will be wiped out. Remember brothers, if only just ten of us volunteer to lay down our lives and take Hari Mishra's beating, that'll make all the difference. Wherever we spill a drop of our blood, the stain will remain forever. Indelible. Come deluge or high water. When our flesh is set on fire the flame will spread in all ten directions. And our bones, hard like iron from Hari Mishra's beatings, will begin to sing wherever they scatter and fall, and they'll never diminish or dwindle to nothingness even if a warrior like Bhima were to grind them against Mount Meru for aeons. They'll continue to sing even if they're thrown into the bottomless depths of the ocean. We aren't really useless, brothers. We're the peasants, farmers, farmhands, labourers. We're the ones that make the dry arid earth yield crops—we're the true sons of the soil.' Out of breath and with eyes brimming with tears, he couldn't go on.

'Well said,' chimed in Ratana Bhoi. 'Our puny little lives—what difference does it make whether we live or die? Isn't there a saying—don't flog a dead horse? Once we remember we're already dead, there's nothing else to be afraid of.'

'Absolutely right,' agreed Jadu Dalei. 'We're already more dead than alive. It can't get any worse. If anything, we can only begin to live again.'

'Will that ever happen?' Rup Jena wanted to know. 'At the moment, it doesn't bother me a bit if there's a corpse stinking in your home.'

Baraju wiped his face with his towel. 'That's our misfortune, our tragedy. That's what I was talking about a moment ago. Folks, tell me now, are we going to unite, are we determined to come to the rescue of another when he needs our help? Tell me now, give me your word.'

They all hung back, nudging one another.

Jadu Dalei could no longer keep silent. 'Folks, this doesn't involve a levy, nobody's going to become poorer, nobody's going to have to fork out money because of it. This is in our hands, this is something we have to build for ourselves: All men are brothers and the whole village is one family. The alternative is that the divisions and conflicts we've lived with until now will continue. Are you ready to come to my aid when I'm caught up in a crisis, and am I to yours? What do you say, Rup Bhai? Is it better to do this, or rub my hands in glee when your house goes up in the flames of discord? Will you herd my bullocks to the cattle pound if they happen to stray into your vegetable patch? Is that what you'd rather do, brother?'

'Have you any doubts about what I'd do?' Rup replied. 'But brother, do you expect everyone to turn over a new leaf overnight? Surely there are naysayers in our midst, people who will prefer to stay outside the fold, beyond the flock.'

'But we can do all it takes to draw them in, can't we? We can coax and cajole, beg them on bended knees—worse comes to worst, we can ostracize them. The lower castes keep away from the untouchables, because apparently they're dirty and live like pigs. And so we'll reject anyone who decides not to do as we ask, to do what we expressly forbid him to do. How will he be any better than an untouchable? The untouchables merely eat rotten meat and drink liquor, but worse than them are those who wish ill of others and conspire to do them harm.'

'I don't think anyone would like to live beyond the fold,' said Jadu. 'Where would he go?'

'So,' Baraju said, 'let's first pick ten volunteers to watch for erring members and bring them back to the fold. Listen, nothing is beyond us human beings, and as long as we have the good of all in mind, we have nothing to fear—beatings, curses, even death. Here, let me jump into the fire first. Choose the remaining nine.'

Jadu, Nidhia, Rup, Netera, Dharama and others stepped forward one by one, until there were ten.

'Good,' said Jadu, 'we've come this far. But nothing's in the hands of humans, it's all in God's.'

'But God operates through humans. Humans are manifestations of Him.'

'True too! As the holy scriptures say, He's all powerful and nothing, not even a blade of grass, stirs without His will.'

'But Baraju Bhai,' said Dharama, 'no matter what you say, I'm not going to put away my knife just yet. I intend to keep it sharpened.'

Baraju laughed. 'Then we'll begin by throwing your knife into the water.'

*

As Banchha and Rup walked back home, Banchha observed, 'Our Baraju Bhai comes across as a pretty educated man! He has a way with words. How well he spoke, how well he marshalled his arguments!'

'It takes a big fool like you to catch on so late,' laughed Rup. 'Baraju was once a land surveyor, remember? If he were a man without an education, would the government have offered him such a plum job?'

10

Suna's wedding was to take place in April. Paddy had to be steamed, parboiled and husked; black gram had to be ground, made into balls and dried in the sun . . . a string of activities. Hara Bou didn't have a moment's respite.

But instead of lending a helping hand, Netramani stubbornly insisted on visiting her parents. 'Send word to my brother.'

Chhakadi looked on helplessly. The family partition seemed inevitable, imminent. He instructed Sania Bhoi to clean a spot in the barnyard for his share of the green-gram harvest. Sania, who eked out a living by working full-time for others for half the year and was a daily wager the rest of the time, was taken by surprise.

'You don't get it, do you?' Chhakadi said.

'Just what're you asking me to do? Why do you want a separate spot?'

'What's it to you? Do as you're told. Does someone buying ginger go enquiring about the price of ships?'

'What the hell are you talking about? What ginger-buyer, what ship prices? I don't understand you at all. You want a family partition, do you? You want to separate from your brother? From Baraju Pradhan of all people? Why, that man's made of pure gold, worth over a 100,000 rupees!'

'Don't let your mouth run away with you, man! Do exactly as you're told. Period.'

Fair enough, Sania thought. After all, I'm just a hired hand, why should I offer an opinion? But is this Chhakadi, this poor specimen worth anything at all? How can the two brothers be so different, Baraju one type and then this one—does he even deserve to be called a human being?

*

On his return home—he had been away for two days looking to buy a bullock—Baraju heard about all this and commented to Hara Bou with a smile, 'That's good, the boy's beginning to think about household matters. Maybe he'll become focused at last! What do you say?'

'And a welcome thing that'd be too,' grinned Hara Bou. 'It'd do no one any harm.' She'd realized by now her husband meant what he said and did what he meant. So it mattered little whether she, Hara Bou, got the drift or not; her role was simply not to contradict her husband.

Baraju questioned Sania. 'Hey, is this the spot being cleaned up for the green-gram harvest this year? In which of our fields will the reaping begin?'

'The five-acre patch.'

'Is it dry yet, the crop?'

'I plan to pull out the plants tomorrow and pile them in your portion of the barnyard.'

'My portion?' Baraju chuckled. 'Who do you think the whole backyard belongs to?'

'God!' Sania groaned. 'Don't you see what's happening? You see it's sandalwood but ask, is that ordinary wood? What you're seeing with your eyes is all there is to see! This portion is Chhakadi's. He's asked me to make it ready for his share. Yours will be piled in a separate heap.'

'What's all this with his share and mine? If his share is separate from mine, then nothing's mine. Pile the entire harvest of green gram on his spot in the barnyard.'

How does one talk sense to a bull-headed man like this? Sania wondered. 'So Chhakadi takes it all?'

'Of course,' Baraju smiled. 'Who else? Until now I was taking it all. Now it's his turn. Who else is there?'

Sania shot him a look of bewilderment. 'There'll be no dividing it up?'

'Has that happened until now? When I took the entire crop, he was part of me. Now when he takes it all, I'm part of him.'

Sania found this all too hard to unravel. He stacked the entire harvest in one pile.

Chhakadi confronted Sania. 'What have you done, stupid man? Why have you put the whole lot in one pile?'

'Baraju asked me to. He said you were to take the whole lot.'

'Nonsense!' said Chhakadi, irritated no end.

'That elder brother of yours,' Sania said, 'he said the entire crop belongs to you.'

What saint would have remained calm in the face of such provocation, Chhakadi thought. Who wouldn't find it testing the limits of his patience? He was looking forward to a smooth split without a hitch, but his plan had hit a snag.

When Netramani heard about it, she said, 'Good. Let him show off all he wants. Let him show off how noble he is. Sell the entire stock of green gram after you've harvested it.'

*

'Nothing could be better,' Hari Mishra gave his opinion. 'Just what the doctor prescribed. Don't miss out on this opportunity.'

'But Uncle,' Chhakadi said, far from happy, 'this is how he'll go on about everything from now on. Meanwhile there'll be one wedding after another, a daughter's today, a son's tomorrow!'

Mishra gave a broad wink. 'You don't take long to cotton on, do you, son! You're truly a pigeon in a brazier's household, aren't you? That's precisely the game that's now afoot.'

Mishra's words of praise made Chhakadi's chest swell with pride. 'I'm not a dimwit, Uncle. I catch on very fast, I do. But that woman of mine's forever harping on what a damn fool I am.'

'If you're a damn fool, then who's smart?'

'All right, Uncle, now that the green-gram issue is settled, what do you think's next?'

'The jaggery, surely?'

'Spot on, Uncle!' Chhakadi laughed. 'Is there anyone who can get the better of you? Is there anything you don't know? Let me fill you in on last year's production. Of the ten or twelve jars of jaggery, I got only two for my shop; the rest my brother stored in his room. Of these he might have sold four or six. The rest he might be saving for the upcoming wedding.'

'But boy, do you have to have every little thing explained to you right down to the dots on the i's? Look, of the twelve jars of jaggery, six were rightfully yours. But you got only two. So how many did you lose? Four, isn't that right? No matter where they're stored, whether inside or out of the home, they're rightfully yours; you can claim them anytime.'

'That's it, Uncle. My woman's been nagging me to go get whatever jars are in my brother's room and bring them to ours.'

'Your little wife—why, she has sense, she knows exactly what advice to give you. After all, she comes from a good family!'

When Chhakadi moved three jars of jaggery from Baraju's room to his, Hara Bou didn't say a word. All she heard from Chhakadi was: 'This is for my shop. Whatever you need for the wedding, you've got to buy.'

When Baraju came home, she mentioned it to him. 'Why did Chhakadi take away the jaggery jars?'

Baraju gave a broad grin—his only response these days, which didn't sit easily on his otherwise heavy, brooding face. 'He may have taken them because we're going to be buying some jaggery for the wedding.'

'What argument is that? How logical is that? Why do we have to buy jaggery when we have our own?'

'How will we get through with the wedding if we don't buy some?'

Hara Bou kept quiet. She was far from convinced, but what could she answer?

*

'But this isn't fair at all,' Sania Bhoi said. 'Not at all. Who tilled the land, who watered it and watched over it at night? But when the time comes to harvest the crop, who takes it all?'

'Chhakadi wouldn't have done this if he had a bit of common sense,' Netera Ojha remarked. 'What man separates from a brother like Baraju? That Chhakadi, he lacks judgement, I tell you. Someone's manipulating him.'

'Would he have done it if he had even a drop of wisdom left? Baraju's the only one who works, the only one who earns, and all his earnings are for the whole family, for everyone's upkeep. Besides, he gave Chhakadi two jars of jaggery for his shop. Did he ask Chhakadi for a share of the profits? And on top of that, Chhakadi makes off with three jars his brother had saved for the wedding. How wrong-minded can one get? Just because he himself doesn't have any children, does he expect everyone else to be childless too?'

*

All Baraju wanted was that nothing happening at home should turn into gossip. He did not realize things had reached the point of no return, that his family was on the verge of splitting up due to outside forces. He felt reassured by his conviction that there would be no partition until he agreed to one. Here he was trying to unite the whole village into one family and make everyone a brother of everyone else, but his own family was on the brink of separating. He remembered his father's last words: Let there be no walls across the courtyard of this homestead or dividing ridges across the paddy fields of this family. Would Baraju not be able to ensure this? What was the point in continuing to live then? What difference was there between life and death?

Only last evening men of all castes in the village, from peasants to untouchables to confectioners to barbers, had shared the consecrated prasad of Goddess Mangala and sworn brotherhood together, and today Baraju and Chhakadi, born of the same parents and sharing the same blood, would split up? Tomorrow Chandara and Jagua would be justified in voicing their misgivings: Since Baraju had failed to preserve the unity of his own family, that of the village was only a mirage. How on earth could one villager treat another as his brother? How could one villager turn up at another's home to look after him if he was taken ill? Would Baraju have to put up with the humiliation as long as he lived? Of what use was his life then? He would be better off dead.

The stem of a jute plant, it is said, breaks but never bends. So it was with Baraju—he was the true son of his father. Suna's wedding, he decided, would be celebrated on the same scale as Hara's, and so would Moti's when her time came. For Hara's wedding, had he been forced to borrow money from outside or draw on reserves he had secreted away? No, every bit of the expenses had come out of the family resources, out of whatever was available at home. So why should he worry his head off when it came to Suna and Moti? Had the poor girls had any choice in their birth, in the choice of their parents? God had decided that for them. He put milk for them in their mother's breasts, He provided for them as He did for everyone else, everyone and everything. Why should he, Baraju, worry and lose precious sleep? As God says in the Bhagavat:

'I alone do everything, and get everything done
Besides me, there's no one.'

If anyone should be troubled it should be He; this was His lookout. Baraju needn't worry. On his deathbed, his father had raised his hands heavenwards and said, 'Son, I'm leaving behind nothing but the virtue and goodness I lived by.' Where did he leave them, with whom? With Baraju or Chhakadi? Or with somebody else? No matter with whom or where, righteousness was for everyone to observe; it dwelt within all living beings, and he, Baraju, need have no fear. Fear was only for those who didn't believe in God, for those who were atheists. There was goodness everywhere and in everything, animate and inanimate—trees and leaves, rivers and hills, sparse woods and dense forests, everywhere, in the crowds of people, as much in villages as in towns, and even in places where there were neither human beings nor animals. Goodness was everywhere. Why should Baraju be afraid? And of whom? There was Dhruba, that mere chit of a boy, who was completely unafraid of the deep forests and ferocious beasts like tigers and bears!

Baraju bowed his head and touched it to the ground: 'Oh God, give me strength and courage to meet vice and vileness, injustice and sin, head-on, whenever and wherever I find them. Even at the cost of my life. May my bones weapons make, the weapons with which to fight sin and vice.'

*

Suna's wedding was celebrated. An expensive sari was bought for Netramani, but she was far from happy. One wedding too many, she grumbled. All the resources of the family would be drained, the coffers emptied, and a sari should placate me? The sari be damned, I've seen enough saris.

Baraju couldn't help losing himself in thought. The stream of humanity. Rushing on down. Since the beginning of time. Human beings constantly trampling on one another, all caught in a mad scramble to get ahead of others, amid the rising cries of those dying or already more than half-dead underfoot; on the move all the while, not pausing a moment to pay heed. Some sinking, others floating along, unconcerned with one another. Waves crashing. Humans still not able to resist the temptation of drinking the blood of their own kind—brothers, kinsmen, relations, neighbours. When would they ever learn, when would they become truly civilized? Jungles and forests had yielded to houses and buildings, but human nature had remained the same—ruled by meanness, jealousy, cruelty and pride. Meanwhile, the earth continued to make its way round the sun and night turned to day—days into months and years. Meanness, jealousy, cruelty and pride reigned unabated; battles and wars were fought; innumerable kings and emperors came and passed; aeons went by, Satya to Treta to Dvapara to Kali now. In the relentless flow of time, who could say where they stood? And poor Baraju—where did he stand? He was no more than a mere straw in the stream, arrested and entangled in whirlpools, all froth and bubbles, stopping for one moment and gone the next. Was someone asking him to stop? Who was it crying out to him—the children of the good earth? A sea of humanity. Oh men, will nothing be enough for you—Earth, the sky and the sea? How can you trample your own people, your own brothers and kinsmen? Some overtaken by disease and moaning for medicine, but without money. Was there nobody to buy some for them? Someone else had only one meal every two days; a young mother had no milk in her breasts to suckle her child; someone else had been beaten black and blue and didn't have a coin to buy two drops of oil to rub into the welts to ease the pain. Oh, doomed race of humanity, pause in your tracks for a moment, will you, and think: so many like you have come and gone, kings and emperors, what's the hurry? Won't you stop for a moment and listen? Isn't someone calling out to you? Can't you hear the voice of another human being? Or do you think the voice you hear is not made by a human being?

He, Baraju Pradhan, had chosen to stop and listen, even as he floated down the stream. Heeding the voices of the sick and the half-dead, of the starving, of the beaten and bruised. What did he have to be afraid of? If need be, he would go begging from door to door; he would receive his share of flogging and lashes too. What did he have to fear death for, when his life wasn't his own to begin with? Who would be bothered if he died? Millions of people lost their lives every day—some to disease, others to thirst, hunger and starvation, some to being beaten like cattle by men like Hari Mishra. No one was listening to their piteous cries, from the moment they were born through to the moment their lives came to an end. Unknown, unnoticed, unsung and unlamented. He, Baraju, was one of them. God, Who controls what happens in the world and before Whom everyone, from kings and emperors to the wretched of the earth, are all the same, why hasn't He given those with riches and strength a bit of pity for the wretched and the have-nots, a little feeling for the poor and the weak? Take Dharama Das, the untouchable. Who filled him with poison? Why, he was dead already, dead from being beaten day in and day out. He was no longer alive, more of a ghost really. Many like him had turned into ghosts even when they were still breathing. God, the upholder of righteousness and goodness, truth and beauty, give them some wisdom. May the rich and the powerful look upon the poor and the weak with compassion. May the poor and the weak shun violence and animosity when they look at the rich and the powerful. May human beings recognize one another as human beings and love and respect one another. May the deprived not think ill of the privileged.

Baraju's eyes brimmed with tears.

'Baraju Bhai! Brother!'

Baraju couldn't get to the door fast enough. 'Nitai, man, what's the matter?'

Nitai Maharana was coated in dust and dirt from head to toe. 'I'm done for, brother,' he bawled. 'My children are out on the street. Where can I get fifty rupees? You know how much I earn from cutting wood. My children are going to starve and die!'

'Come on, brother. Get a grip on yourself and tell me what's happened.'

Nitai slumped down on Baraju's veranda, cupping his head in his hands. 'I borrowed ten rupees from Hari Mishra for my daughter's wedding and have already paid back all of twenty. But today, when I went to Mishra to ask him to return the promissory note I signed, he said I still owed him fifty. Where will I get fifty rupees? As you know, I'm dirt poor and own no land, no property. You know what he said? "Why don't you get some backer of yours to pay up for you? Don't I know the whole lot of you have ganged up against me?" My wits deserted me when I heard these words. My insides roiled and knotted. Until now my kids had been able to survive on rice water, but now they'll be out on the street, they'll simply perish. Where will I find the money, I who have no money to buy medicine for my youngest child who's been coughing out his little lungs for the last three months?' He began to howl again.

'Hari Mishra said you still owe him money? Didn't you give him the dates and details of the payments you'd made?'

'Brother, what can I tell you? I rolled in the dust until all the hair on my head fell out, but Hari Mishra wouldn't listen. His only response was, "Since you all have ganged up against me, go get one of them to pick up the tab!"'

'Calm down, Nitai, calm down. Have patience. Injustice can't be allowed to win.'

'Brother, I tell you, it's finished with me. There's no one to look after me, except the One up there Who makes day and night. It's all up to Him now.'

Baraju's eyes smarted with tears, his lips quivered. 'You're right, Nitai. It's He Who controls everything. He makes day and night, up there and down here too. He keeps an eye on everything, and He'll look after you too.' Tears streamed down his eyes. Who else would, if not He? Would Baraju? Could he, even if he wanted to? He was too poor—he didn't amount to much. In the end, He who created Nitai Maharana and Hari Mishra would see to everything.

'I alone do everything, and get everything done
Besides me, there's no one.'

What could poor Baraju Pradhan now do? It was all God's will, His wishes. But He could express them through Baraju Pradhan.

11

On Suna's wedding day, Netramani refused to wear the sari bought for her.

Chhakadi's store was doing good business, selling not only jaggery and green gram but also other items. With the money he bought Netramani a necklace and pair of anklets.

Baraju had to purchase all the items for his daughter's wedding, including green gram and jaggery, from another shop.

Chhakadi went and met Hari Mishra. 'Uncle, what do I do now—my brother's not reacting to anything I do, not even when I'm at my meanest, totally insufferable. I sold off the entire harvest of green gram this year, the entire stock of jaggery, but he didn't make a comment. Not just he; that blessed wife of his didn't utter a word either. But my woman, she doesn't stop nagging: "Let's split, before it's too late; they've a whole brood of children to raise and marry off, that's why they're keeping quiet. Lying low's to their advantage, don't you see? Moti's still to be married off, and who's keeping account of things being quietly smuggled off to the homes of the girls already married off? The boy consumes half a seer of milk a day, not a drop less!" But Uncle, none of this seems right to me. Not at all. I wish my brother would protest, say something. In the past, my sister-in-law was quick to take offence, but of late she's become silent. Talk of miracles! How do I act against those who won't fight back? How do I bicker over nothing? What'll people say if I do? But my wife, she says to hell with what others think, let them say what they want, good or bad, and as much as they please, are they going to share anything with us?'

'Exactly my thoughts!' Hari Mishra said. 'As usual, your wife's absolutely right! She has good common sense. After all, she's from a respectable family. But you, my boy, you're still the nitwit you were. Say, why're you bothered about how people will talk? Do wretches and lowlifes matter? Do they have a kind word for me? But does it bother me a bit if they praise or condemn me? For all I care, they can go on barking like a pack of dogs.'

But Chhakadi remained unconvinced. 'I understand, Uncle, I do, but somehow all this makes me uncomfortable. When my brother says "yes" to everything I propose, how do I force a partition? Tell him to separate, to cook and eat separately?'

'Cooking and eating separately are no big deal, boy. That's a solution for women. You eat separately for a few days, and then bury the hatchet and get together again. Just a farce, if you ask me. Partition's the real solution, and a manly one at that. Partition or nothing. Complete division of assets—land, cattle, cooking utensils. What's the point of removing a pot from the kitchen today and putting it back tomorrow or the day after? That's how women behave. Shameful, if you ask me.'

'I'm at my wits' end. I can no longer think straight. My wife's after me to start with eating separately. Let's divide the cooking utensils first, she says, then we'll graduate to land, property and cattle, but they have to produce the full details of the two previous wedding expenses and deduct them from their share of the property.'

'Chhakadi,' Hari Mishra said. 'You're one lucky dog. Not everyone's as fortunate to have as wise a wife as yours. She always comes out with the smartest advice, exactly what the occasion demands. But you seem to be dithering. Why're you so confused? Where's the room for confusion? Why don't you go ask five elders from the area to mediate and divide up your land, homestead and everything? Get your rightful share and be done with it once and for all. What part of all this is so baffling to you?'

'You're right, Uncle. And let me tell you something, when it comes to partition I'll rely on you; you're better than any wise elder around. The only hitch is how I can suddenly spring it on my brother, since I've never raised the subject with him.'

'Who can teach you, silly boy? If you can't muster the courage to talk to your brother, if all you can do is keep mum, then go bury yourself in your corner of the house and forget your future.' Hari Mishra was exasperated.

'That woman of mine, Uncle, she's not giving me a moment's peace. No, no, I'm asking you to come to our place as soon as tomorrow. Uncle, until you come, nothing will get going.'

'Come on, what can I do if you refuse to open your mouth in your elder brother's august presence? Is it my business to advise people to push for partitions? Is that what you're asking from me?'

'No. It's just that I'm not a total nitwit. I'm going to have it out with my brother tonight.'

*

Chhakadi had showed off in front of Hari Mishra, but when he reached home in the afternoon, he couldn't raise the issue. He found Baraju on the veranda copying the tenth canto of the Bhagavat on palm leaves with an iron stylus. Their father Shyam Pradhan had done up to the fourth canto and left it to Baraju to complete the job, like a father laying the foundations of a temple and leaving it to his son to place the spire on the top.

Barju was so immersed in his work he had eyes for nothing else. Chhakadi hung around for a while, but left when he didn't gain his brother's attention.

He was in a terrible fix: How was he going to bring up the topic? He fidgeted, rushed in and out of his room, paced the courtyard and consulted Netramani. 'Listen, brother's alone at the moment. Should I speak to him now? Is this the right time, do you think?'

'Do you have to ask my opinion about everything?' she replied with a frown.

Chhakadi went out to the veranda again. Baraju was as engrossed as before, unaware his brother had made several trips there. In a shameful dither, the boy crept back to his room once again and called out to his wife. 'All right, tell me what exactly I should tell brother.'

Netramani rolled her eyes in exasperation. 'Get lost. Don't be such a coward.'

Even my wife dares humiliate me, Chhakadi thought, as he walked back to the veranda again. Enough was enough, it was time now to take the bull by the horns.

'Brother,' he called out to Baraju.

Baraju stopped working and raised his head. 'Wanting to speak to me, are you?'

Chhakadi lapsed into a stammer. 'Oh no! I was just passing this way.' He couldn't make himself scarce fast enough.

Baraju plunged back into his work.

Chhakadi had carted away the entire green gram harvest, he had carted away the entire jaggery production, but he hadn't had to argue with his brother because Baraju had remained completely silent. So how would he bring up the topic of family partition? Everybody loved to call him a coward, a spineless weakling—but did anyone come forward to mention the matter to Baraju?

*

The next day, in the early morning, Baraju went to lift water and irrigate their land. It was just the end of Kartik, but the rains had suddenly withdrawn and water had become acutely scarce. Where could a farmer turn when the shortage was decided by the heavens? As the saying goes, diseases might bubble up from within, but misfortune always rains down from the skies.

Baraju Pradhan was busy at work with Sania Bhoi, irrigating his field. From all around came floating snatches of the songs, chatter and babble of people engaged in a similar enterprise. The morning star was still shining, reflected in the waters. Dawn was about to break: outlines of the surrounding villages could be made out. Clusters of trees too. Flocks of egrets could be seen settled like white dots on empty paddy fields, ready to spear worms with their beaks. Crows, mynahs, kites and cranes were in flight, their raucous cacophony filling the sky. The eastern horizon was breaking out in patches of red. A border of mist clung to the distant villages like a sheet of white.

After watering the land, Baraju headed home with a bundle of grass balanced on his head. The short piece of cloth he wore around his waist was wet from the dewy ears of corn. When he reached home, he found Hari Mishra on his doorstep chatting with Chhakadi.

'Son,' Hari Mishra said, as soon as he saw him. 'Have you given up sleeping at night? You're an impossible man. You can't stay away from work, can you?'

'What has made you pay us a dawn visit, Uncle?' Baraju headed for the cowshed to unload the bundle of grass.

'Your brother, Chhakadi, won't give me a moment of peace,' Mishra said. 'He's after me all the time. Seems there's a family partition to be mediated here, and he can't do without my good offices. Now, I'm a busy man and have so many things to attend to besides.'

Baraju's eyes widened. 'Who wants a partition, Uncle? Who wants a partition from whom? I just don't get it.'

Mishra was baffled. 'What, you don't know anything about it? Has this boy been telling me stories? Impossible! For the last three months he's been after me: "Uncle, you must come over, I need you to mediate and arbitrate, we're having a partition." I fended him off as long as I could: "Come on, you're too young to force a family partition." But he was past listening to sound advice and kept on whining: "No, you don't understand, Uncle, my brother has already spent a big chunk of the family funds getting two of his daughters married, and we haven't inherited an enormous fortune. I can't take the pressure any longer. I want my share, and brother has to produce the details of the wedding expenses so that his can be reduced by that amount. After that he's on his own and I'm on mine." The boy hasn't given me a moment's rest, I tell you. So what could I do in the end? I had to turn up here, and morning's the best time. I'm sure there'll be at least three persons hanging around my door waiting for me when I get back. There're matters to wrap up in as many as three different villages too, family feuds to sort out—God, all these responsibilities have stretched me so thin I've begun to neglect my own affairs. My farms and plots are beginning to dry up because there's no one to oversee their being watered on time.' Mishra might trumpet as much as he liked that his valuable and precious time was being wasted settling the problems of others, but the truth was he made a lot of money from these disputes. He who raised the wick of the oil lamp had his fingers greased.

Baraju laughed. 'So the boy has been pestering you and wasting your precious time over a trivial issue like this?

A family partition, a division of family assets—is that such a difficult matter? Uncle, go on, you've got better things to do. Chhakadi's a silly, mindless boy. What made you take him seriously?'

'Would he listen to what I told him to show him the error in his thinking? He was downright adamant: "Uncle, you're like a father to me, I can't find my way around the matter if you don't help me." Ask him.'

'No one's denying what you're saying,' said Baraju. 'But he's wasted your valuable time and got you to rush here for nothing. Such a trivial matter . . .'

'It's not a crime he's committed,' Hari Mishra said, rising to his feet and gently hitting his legs with his towel. 'Was he wrong to get me over here? I don't think so. What do you say, Chhakadi my boy?' He turned around. 'Oh God, where has he disappeared to? It's his affairs we're discussing and he's gone and done a vanishing trick!'

Chhakadi had made himself scarce as soon as he saw his brother approaching. He was feeling as guilty as a thief.

Vexed by the boy's conduct, Hari Mishra returned home in a huff. What a gutless little fool, that Chhakadi. Mishra had made himself vulnerable for nothing.

*

It finally became clear to Baraju that Chhakadi was hell-bent on a partition, that he would stop at nothing. But he too was determined: Let's see how the boy will force the split, how he'll push for a partition and break up the family! That'll never happen as long as Baraju Pradhan is alive and kicking.

He called Chhakadi, took him aside and spoke to him. 'Why're you inviting outsiders to meddle in our affairs, to mediate our division of property? But first of all, tell me why you want a partition so badly.'

Not for nothing had Netramani coached Chhakadi for months and had him learn his lines by heart. Not for nothing had Hari Mishra worked on him and imparted so much of his worldly wisdom. He mustered his courage, and put on a brave front. 'Why shouldn't I want a family partition?' he answered. 'All the family income has been spent on your two daughters' weddings and feeding your children. How long can I put up with that?'

Baraju was stunned. Was this the same Chhakadi who had never before raised his head in front of him? This must be someone else in Chhakadi's guise! 'All right, so you want a partition. But do you know what I want? No partition. I want nothing split in half—not the house, not the land, not the cattle, not anything. So you tell me how our conflicting wishes can be reconciled.' He was beaming.

Chhakadi was confused, and his face fell. 'I don't understand such complications. We split everything in half and put an end to all squabbles and quarrels. Why're you splitting hairs?'

'But nothing should be divided; on that I insist. Everything must remain as it is—whole, as before.'

Chhakadi's irritation mounted. 'But I'm telling you I can no longer live with you.'

'I'm not against living apart; by all means, let's live apart. But let's not divide the property. That way both our wishes will be met.'

'You're complicating matters. Your words are confusing me. Let's total up the wedding expenses of the two girls and all other expenses, and have a fair division of the property.'

Baraju gave a laugh. 'Wedding expenses? Come on, you fool. Who's going to be able to figure out all those details now? Did we think to keep strict accounts of the expenses so we could raise them at the time of a family partition? And I'm telling you this: Let there be no walls, ridges, fences, divisions. Let's only take our meals separately. The house, the land, the vegetable patches and gardens are all yours. From now on, they belong entirely to you. What do I need them for? I've only Moti to marry off. The young Dama can earn a living as a farmhand, which leaves the two of us, my wife and me, to fend for ourselves. We'll manage somehow. No problem.'

Chhakadi was left speechless. Swallowing his spit, he stared at his brother. He would never understand this man. 'Explain that again. What did you say?'

'Don't you understand?' Baraju laughed. 'No division of property, but we'll live separately. Everything's yours—the homestead, the land and cattle, everything. Tomorrow I'll leave with my family. Do you understand now?'

Chhakadi didn't know whether to laugh or cry. His gaze was riveted on his brother, but after a while he wasn't sure if this was his brother or someone else. 'No,' he mumbled, before lapsing into silence, 'I don't.'

'All this is yours. They're your property. Tomorrow morning I'll leave with Dama, Moti and their mother.'

'No!' Chhakadi mumbled once again.

He wasn't just paying lip service this time—the cry had come from deep within, not produced under pressure from Netramani or through Hari Mishra's persuasion. Just a simple and straightforward 'no' from the recesses of his heart.

Rushing inside, Baraju sought out his wife. 'Let's see how ready you are to respond to the call, which has come at last,' he said with a smile. 'The other day you were full of firm resolves, pledges and promises. Tomorrow morning we're going to walk off, leaving everything behind. Will you rise to the occasion?'

Hara Bou couldn't believe her ears. 'Come on, don't you try to trick me!'

'Have I ever done that? Why would I try such a thing now, Hara Bou? Have I ever told you a lie?'

But his wife was unconvinced. 'Where will you live if you leave here?'

Baraju gave a laugh. 'Where to live? Well, do people decide that ahead of time when they decide to leave home suddenly?'

'But without deciding that, how can you leave your home? Are you possessed by a ghost? What kind of talk is this?'

'I'm leaving here tomorrow morning, Hara Bou. If you wish to leave with me, you'd better start packing.'

What option did she have? 'All right, tell me what you wish to take with you, and I'll start packing.'

'Take nothing, neither a kitten nor a counterfeit coin. Just a change of clothes, just what we can carry.'

'What about utensils?'

'Nothing. And another thing. Don't tell anyone.'

'As if I had nothing better to do!'

*

Chhakadi filled Netramani in on the developments.

'My, what's the big deal?' she asked. 'Do they think that'll scare the daylights out of us? What kind of a threat's that anyway? Do they themselves take it seriously? As if people who threaten to leave home actually do! The whole family gorges on whatever's at home, but when it comes to sulking they put on a good show. All right, let them leave. Do they think people will run after them begging them not to go? Empty threats are all they're capable of!'

She then proceeded to take out her anger on her husband. 'You little coward, why did you run from him like a thief? Why didn't you call his bluff? Why didn't you tell him point blank: So go, don't simply threaten to. Let me see you do that. Instead of standing your ground like a man and having it out with him, you ran away with your tail tucked between your legs.'

'Stop working yourself into a froth, woman' Chhakadi said with disgust. 'Wait until tomorrow morning and see. He vowed to go away. Keep quiet until then. It can do us no harm.'

'All right,' Netramani capitulated. 'But why didn't you take him up on his dare and tell him to get lost?'

Through the thin wall Baraju heard every word she was yelling at the top of her voice.

12

The next day dawned like any other. Baraju roused Chhakadi in the small hours to explain to him where the plots, paddy fields and vegetable patches were located, which cattle were theirs, the details of the stock of paddy and cereals preserved at home for the next sowing. All this didn't take more than an hour—their property wasn't large.

'There. Now you've got the whole picture,' Baraju said. 'So, shall we separate?'

'That's it,' grunted Chhakadi. 'Just divide it all up equally, half and half.'

'Don't imagine I've something up my sleeve when I say no to that. Our father's last wish was the property not be divided.'

'Then do as you please,' Chhakadi said, not masking his rising irritation. 'Who can talk you out of what you've decided?'

When Baraju went inside, he found his wife making a tidy bundle of clothes, pots and pans and other household items. 'What're you up to?'

'Aren't we taking these with us?'

'Who told you to pack so many things? I said not to take the brass utensils. And why're you obsessed with these pots and pans?'

'But I bought them with my own money!' She began to sulk.

'Put them back. Right now. You bought them with your money—huh? Undo everything. Take only a few pieces of clothing, and even those you have to show to the younger daughter-in-law before packing them.'

Hara Bou looked up at her husband. He was all smiles. She began to smile too. They seemed to understand each other—words were no longer necessary.

*

Although Hara Bou hadn't breathed a word to a soul, the news of their leaving had eddied around the village and beyond in no time. Several women—among them Saradi Bou, Nandi the Pandit's widow, Netera's mother, Sister Sobha—arrived. One was holding a green twig to brush her teeth, another a little round ball of turmeric paste, yet another a small bowl of oil. One even had a half-smoked cigar wrapped in a banana leaf. 'Shame on you for leaving your own home! What logic is there in that? Surely you wouldn't choose to eat off shards the rest of your life just because a thief has stolen your utensils! A division of property would have been ideal. When sons in a family fall apart and don't wish to live together, they always go for a partition. That happens everywhere, in every home.

But what's happening here is beyond belief! Why must one son walk away from his ancestral place just like that?'

A group of men—Jadu, Nidhia, Dharama and Magunia among them—collected in front of the Pradhan house. Nidhia wiped away his tears with his towel. 'No one can make Baraju Bhai change his mind. He'll not change course once he's decided to do something. He's like the wheels of the Rukuna chariot—they never roll backwards!'

'But how can Baraju Bhai walk off leaving us all behind?' Dharama wailed.

'But what can you do to stop him?' Jadu laughed.

'What can I do? Well, for one thing I can follow him, walk in his footsteps, go with him wherever he's headed. He's leaving everything behind, but what do I own that would tie me down here?'

Maga pitched in. 'Dharama's right. What's the point of sticking to this miserable little village any longer? The old Pradhan's long gone, now Baraju Bhai is leaving. What seeds have we planted here that will grow into trees and bear fruit for us? We all might as well leave this place.'

'No point in dabbling in words,' Dharama said. 'Let's decide about this. Shall we simply look on while a family is being forced out of its home and hearth?'

Jadu Dalei mocked him. 'But Dharama, first tell us what you can do to prevent it.'

'Why, let five of us sit together here and supervise a fair family partition. That won't take much time. And that Chhakadi Pradhan, it wouldn't take more than two words to convince him. He won't be able to agree fast enough to whatever arrangement we hammer out! Brother, I'm Dharama Das, not a nobody!'

'You're working yourself into a fine froth for nothing,' answered Nidhia. 'Baraju Bhai's leaving home on his own initiative. He doesn't want a family partition. How can you force one on him? Will that be easy?'

'But will it be any easier if we let him just up and leave? Are we all just silent ghosts around here?'

'A vintage Gopalpur bigmouth, that's what you are!'

'Come on, wiseacre!'

Nidhia was on the verge of making a cutting retort, when Jadu Dalei stopped him. 'Oh, shut the hell up. Why're you all wasting your breath?'

Baraju was appalled the news had made it around the village. But leave he would, no matter what. Since he had first heard his brother talk of partition, since the time the accounts of Hara's wedding expenses were demanded, his mind had been made up. He had never bothered to keep accounts. The quantities of produce from the fields— everything was for the whole family. No, it was time to go. The ancestral home did have its appeal, but his brother had been plotting a partition for so long! Enough was enough. The words of his younger brother's wife echoed in his ears: 'Leave by all means if you wish! What's holding you back?' No, he could no longer continue to live in this place.

'Come on,' he told his wife. 'Time we hit the road.'

Meanwhile the women hadn't given Hara Bou a break. 'Look Hara Bou, what kind of stupidity is this? Whoever's heard of anything like it? As a young woman, how can you roam around here, there and everywhere? Has such a thing ever happened elsewhere, in any other village? Why didn't you give a flat "no" to Baraju when he first broached the idea?'

'As if he would've heeded me,' Hara Bou laughed. 'Does anyone take what I have to say into consideration, listen to my opinion?'

'But how will you be able to roam here and there?' Sister Sobha persisted. 'You're a young woman after all. And you aren't low caste. You're a farmer's wife, not an untouchable's!'

Saradi Bou snorted. 'What're you saying? Daughters and wives from respectable families have already come out of their homes. They're going to the market and taking walks out in the open. So Hara Bou won't be committing a sin if she does that.'

In Chhakadi's bedroom, the younger daughter-in-law Netramani and the Pandit's widow, whispering without end, were laughing uncontrollably.

'Delay no longer,' Baraju said, lifting the bundle of clothes and wrapping his towel around his head. Then he picked up his stick, three hands in length, and strode out of the house.

Hara Bou followed him, her son on her hip, holding Moti by the hand and smiling at the village women. She didn't look back. Nothing she was leaving behind—the boxes, the pots and pans, the patches where she had grown vegetables and chillies—held any attraction. What a strange woman!

Maga, Netera, Chandara, Dharama and the whole lot had thought they would make Baraju change his mind, but now they were beyond hope.

'It'd be a waste of breath,' said Jadu, with a sigh. 'Not even Brahma, Vishnu and Maheshwar could make him change his mind. So, let's wish him well. May he succeed in doing whatever he's decided. Let's not waste our time on something that won't do any good.'

Someone quoted from the Bhagavat:

'A man who puts up with all his bodily discomfort and pain
Is like a python in the forest.'

'True,' remarked someone else. 'A man putting up with bodily pain and discomfort—but does Baraju Bhai bother about his body?'

'If only he had a fixed address!' said Nidhia. 'God! Here today, elsewhere tomorrow! That's too much.'

'But now his home is everywhere!' said Jadu. 'He doesn't have to think about any one place any more. A man who gives up his ancestral place so calmly—what cares does he have? Does he even worry about where his next meal is coming from? As the Bhagavat says:

"He does not discriminate between good and bad
And welcomes whatever comes his way, from wherever."'

A smiling Baraju walked on, stick in hand, trailed by his wife, Hara Bou. Holding Moti's hand in hers and baby Dama on her hip, she nodded and smiled at the village women.

Baraju noticed Jadu. 'Brother Jadu, do look after the village, don't forget.'

'How can I, all by myself?'

'Come on, the same tired old litany. When are you ever alone? Look at me, am I alone now? Remember those lines from the Bhagavat?

"I am the One Who is the mover, I get things done
Besides Me, there's none other."'

Indeed nobody was alone, Jadu mused. Neither he, Jadu, nor Baraju either. No man is alone, somebody is walking along with him, giving him company, and as long as he has God's company what are his worries, what does he fear?

Jadu wiped his eyes.

To them all—Dharama, Nidhia, Maga, Netera, everyone—Baraju bid farewell. 'Stay well, brothers. Stop worrying. There's God to take care of everything. I'll always be thinking of you people, wherever I go. I'll always be making enquiries about you.'

The men all seemed imbued with a profound sense of respect and reverence for Baraju. They had carefully rehearsed what to say to keep him from leaving, made plans to hold him back, but at this last moment they had all become quiet and had simply followed Baraju like a flock of sheep.

Hara Bou had always been bashful when outdoors, and she now felt terribly flustered: the place was crawling with men. How could she stride down the village path to keep up with her husband? A child on her hip, with the end of her sari pulled low over her head, and dragging a daughter by the hand, she was at a great disadvantage. And all those women, especially the newly married ones, staring at her from behind half-open doors and windows. The children, huddled on their verandas, could not make sense of what was happening and were staring and batting their eyelids uncomprehendingly at Dama and Moti.

An old man, his hands and legs stick-thin from disease and starvation, called out from his veranda, 'What's happening to this village—is dharma deserting it today?'

With folded hands and a bow but without breaking his stride, Baraju greeted the old and the elderly he met on his way. He seemed not to have a care in the world. He walked as jauntily as would a man who had stumbled upon a mound of gold, like someone who had become a millionaire overnight.

When he reached the edge of the village, he stopped and once again took leave of all who had tagged along, with a back slap here, a smile there.

Those working in the fields—swarthy earthy beings, sons of the soil—left their work and rushed to him. Some greeted him with a bowed head, others fell at his feet and still others wept inconsolably. In turn, Baraju showed his respect to his seniors and gave his blessings to the youngsters. Then he quickened his pace. A single stride of his counted for three steps by others'.

'Don't walk so fast,' called Hara Bou from behind. 'Moti isn't able to keep up.'

Baraju looked over his shoulder and laughed. 'Why not admit you aren't able to keep pace? Why blame poor Moti? Hey, but did you remember to say goodbye to Chhakadi's wife? I looked for Chhakadi in the crowd, but didn't see him.'

'Oh yes. I spoke to her before leaving, but she remained as silent as a clam. Nor would she look up at me. I don't know what else I could have done.'

Sensing someone was desperately trying to catch up with him, Baraju looked back over his shoulder. The man was panting, all out of breath.

'Gaura, is that you?' Baraju asked. 'Where're you headed?'

Gauranga Sena of Haripur, a quiet contemplative man and friend of Baraju, thought no end of him. He would always seek him out and convince him to take part in dissolving a dispute or preventing a fight among the men of his village. He couldn't bear to stay away from him for long and would come calling at least once a week, sometimes just to say hello. Exchanging a greeting with Baraju was enough. And he never turned up empty-handed; he always came with something: vegetables, aubergines, cucumbers, whatever. An hour of conversation was a must. Sometimes he would stay back to have lunch with Baraju.

'I've been following you right from your doorstep,' Gauranga said, stumbling on his words, his eyes red and puffy from crying. 'Brother, will you promise to do as I ask?'

'What's that?' Baraju looked him in the eye.

'I'll tell you only if you promise to respect my wishes.'

'First tell me what you want.'

'No, give me your word first.' Gauranga knew Baraju inside out. You couldn't pin him down unless you got him to commit beforehand. Once he had given his word, there would be no going back.

Gaura started begging like a child. 'Promise not to turn me down.'

Baraju gave up. 'Why do you think I have to keep my word every time I give it? Am I King Harishchandra or what? Never mind. Come on, out with it now. All right, I give my word.'

Gaura was delighted. 'Brother, come and stay with me for four days. Just four days. Not one day more. Afterwards you may go wherever you please.'

'Let me tell you something—'

'I won't listen to anything! You've given your word. Now it's up to you if you break your promise.' Gaura broke into convulsive sobs like a child.

*

Chhakadi had been off to the market in Nagpur since early morning, right after his brother's briefing, wondering whether Baraju would ever really walk away from home. Both his wife Netramani and Hari Mishra were certain this was just an empty threat and totally unimaginable: Did people simply pack up and leave, forgetting about their property? Leave home just because they didn't get on with their brother? But of course they did, remembered

Chhakadi. Didn't Ram do precisely that? That's one. Didn't he give up his gilded throne, didn't he anoint his brother Bharat as king and install him in his place? One might argue that that happened in another aeon and that things were vastly different now. Now a man would happily slit his brother's throat for the smallest gain. Why, just the other day some zamindar's son slashed the throats of his brother, his brother's wife and children over some property. Netramani was right—it was an empty threat. No man was going to leave his share of property to his brother and walk away. But Baraju was such a strange man, so unpredictable. One just didn't know what to make of him.

Chhakadi could not concentrate on the job at hand, assailed by doubts and misgivings the whole time. Then he ran into Ucchhaba Bhoi, who told him Baraju and his wife and children had already left the village.

He became speechless when he heard this. Had his elder brother really, really left home for good, never to return? What nonsense was that? And how could his wife walk off with him? And Moti and Dama too?

'And who carried their luggage for them?'

'What luggage? Do you think they've gone to see some relations? Or on a pleasure trip? The husband walked on ahead, the wife followed with the children in tow. Mind you, she had one child on her hip and the other dangling from her hand. And the shameless husband was all smiles too! Never heard or seen anything like this before.'

'Which way were they headed? How far could they have gone? In which direction—towards Cuttack?'

'Why? Are you planning to run and stop them? To bring them back? Plenty of people tried to get Baraju to change his mind, but to no avail.'

'Tell me, do people leave home just like that?'

'You're asking me, boy? You saw it with your own eyes. This Baraju fellow just did that.'

'Never mind. He'll be back in a few days. He will. Won't he?'

'How should I know? You're family, you must know better.'

Ucchhaba was anxious to get on with his shopping.

'Hang on, Ucchhaba,' Chhakadi begged him. 'Wait a moment. Did my brother say anything about me when he was leaving?'

'As if I had no better business than to hang around and eavesdrop!' sneered Ucchhaba. 'Let me hurry up and do my shopping. The market's shutting down.'

'Just one more moment, Ucchhaba. In the name of your son, wait!'

Ucchhaba threw him an angry look. 'What kind of a man are you? Didn't I say I didn't overhear anything about you? Now you want me to swear in the name of my son, by God? To tell you what?'

Dejected, Chhakadi trudged back home. On the way he ran into several people who questioned him and gave him an earful too. But in his mind he kept running over what Hari Mishra had once told him: 'The scum will always preach lofty sermons, but will they ever come and fill your house with wealth?'

When he reached home, he found it deathly quiet. The children, Moti and Dama, were not playing in the front yard with sand and coconut shells. No elder brother was on the veranda copying the Bhagavat or twirling twine to make a length of rope. When he walked inside, his heart felt heavy. Not a sound anywhere.

Netramani was busy tidying up. She was now the mistress of the house, with no one around to interfere with her or go against her wishes! No husband's elder brother to keep a social distance from, no elder sister-in-law to fight with. Now her fiat would be command, her word would be the law. She owned the place.

'Did you consider it convenient to finally return home?' she said, all smiles. 'I've been all by myself all this time. Things are still lying scattered all over the place.'

Netramani's words struck him as so offensive that suddenly he began to resent her. Go do everything by yourself, he berated her in silence, now that you own the place, everything, all of it. 'So those people, those who left—are they coming back or not?'

'Why don't you run and get them back?' she said, as she busied herself restoring order to the chaos of winnowing fans, baskets, sacks and pots.

Chhakadi ate a little something and paced the courtyard. The house felt empty and eerie. My brother will surely come back, he thought. He will. For sure. Where will he take shelter and for how long? He isn't alone, he has his wife and children with him. Surely he can't stay away for long!

He paced restlessly between his room and the courtyard, feeling utterly miserable. Big brother will come back. Surely he will. Yes, he will. Yes.

'Why're you pacing the floor?' Netramani admonished him. 'Why don't you open your brother's room and see what he's left behind? Put everything in its proper place. Did he hand over the key to his room before leaving?'

'Stop it, woman. Stop bothering me. Don't you understand he's left everything and gone? No one's carrying off our things. His room's under lock and key, and we've all the time on earth to open it and take a look around.'

'Don't get into a huff, man. If you're so upset, why don't you run and catch up with him?'

'What do you suspect he's stolen? You want to check everything right now, do you, huh?'

'Why would he carry away anything when all could see? And what—a winnowing fan, a clay pot? Whatever he wanted to take he took beforehand, on the sly. Not openly, not in the public glare.'

Chhakadi's depression deepened. His brother had shown him everything—the bundle of clothes, the bags, the betel pouch. There wasn't a coin in any of these. Only in the box was there some money—five rupees and some small change, worth maybe four annas. So why accuse him of spiriting away a vast fortune?

'Did you expect him to stick a finger in your eye and say, "Look here, my dear younger brother, look how good I am at running off with your money!" Just wait, my man, have a little patience. Before four days have passed you'll

get news of your brother settling down somewhere with
a house, land, a vegetable patch and an orchard. Have a
little patience.'

*

Chhakadi was patient. One day passed, then another, and
then yet another. Three days went by without any news.
Jaga Sethi had mentioned that Baraju had gone to Haripur
to Gauranga Sena's place. Could he possibly spend so many
days at Gauranga's? One, two, three days. He found his own
home increasingly oppressive. He had no peace of mind,
whether inside or out. He was so restless. Sometimes he
found fault with Baraju. What was the point of leaving home
in a huff, like one possessed? If he had put his foot down
against partition, wouldn't he, Chhakadi, have fallen in line?

Chhakadi didn't feel he himself had done anything
wrong.

The midday heat was unbearable. Chhakadi had his
lunch. He felt the urge to take the key and unlock his
brother's room. But how could he open and enter the room
that had once belonged to his brother? What was in there?
In broad daylight, he began to be overcome with fear.

A female dove began calling to her chick from a mango
tree in the backyard of the house: 'The measure of grain is
full again, son. Wake up, come back to life, come back from
the dead.' A raven perched on the thatch of the roof had
taken to hourly cawing. Chhakadi's depression deepened.
He felt tortured by memories of his parents and brother.

How different the home had felt then. And now? Who did this house belong to? Who owned the land and the fields? It was all so baffling. There was only darkness all around. The bile of bitterness rose within him.

When he opened his brother's room, he found it tidy, not a thing out of place. The box sat where it had before, intact, not tampered with. The sleeping mats were neatly rolled up leaned against the wall. How he wished the white ants had shredded them! How he wished the room was totally empty—of everything, including the grain sacks and bags, the pots and pans! That would have been so comforting!

His brother had taken nothing with him. Everything was where it should be—the mats, the sheets, the boxes, the utensils. He rummaged everywhere, as if he had lost something, as if the missing object might be lying under the cot or up on the loft. Then his eyes fell on the rubber swan that squeaked when squeezed. He picked it up and pressed it to his heart. Torrents of tears began to roll down his cheeks. Chhakadi, oh poor Chhakadi! Who will enjoy all this property now, with all of them gone? They were eating everything up, were they?

He looked at the rubber swan. He could see hands of children stretching towards the toy. His tears completely blinded him.

Chhakadi wouldn't look up at Netramani, let alone smile or speak normally to her. Tears flowed from his eyes incessantly, no matter where he was. Watching him, his wife felt excited: Never mind these bouts of crying, he was always a bit of a cry baby. He would be all right in a day or two. Once he got over the pangs of parting, he would be his former self.

Chhakadi didn't go to open his shop in the evening. He remained glued to the veranda, tense and silent.

Sadhua Ma walked by, a few twigs in her hand, her threadbare sari pulled over her wrinkled skin. One of the oldest women of the village—no one knew how old she really was—she was mumbling aloud: 'Oh God, is this what You had in mind, this unsightly thing for a godly man? What harm did he ever do anyone? Such a decent man, his head always bowed, never wanting to hurt a fly, never trying to fish in troubled waters! Will this village know another like him? Will there ever be another like him? Had the old Pradhan woman been alive she'd have agreed with me. Poor thing, she could never mention her own son's name because he'd been named after her father-in-law—Baraju!' The old woman's eyes were dry, because all her tears had long dried up. Still she wiped her moist eyelashes with the end of her tattered sari.

Chhakadi rushed inside. 'Brother, brother!' Was he going mad?

When he sat down to dinner at night the tears from his eyes fell on the plate and soaked the rice. When he went to bed he spoke in his sleep: 'Brother, brother!' When he awoke, he couldn't make out what Netramani was telling him. To all her questions he gave the same short answer: 'Yes'. He was no longer himself.

The next morning he was missing. Netramani woke up and found him gone. Hours passed. Midday, then evening, came and went. People looked for him everywhere, but he had left no trace.

But he had not disappeared. He had only gone to Gauranga Sena's place and was sitting on his doorstep. When Dama saw him he ran back into the house, screaming for his mother: 'Mother, come and see who's here—Uncle!'

Baraju hurried out and found his brother sitting on the steps. 'Come inside,' he said. 'Why're you sitting here?'

When they were inside the house, Baraju asked him, 'So what brings you here?'

'I'm joining you,' Chhakadi said in a small voice. 'I'm coming with you.'

'Coming with me where?'

'Wherever you're headed.' Tears streamed down his cheeks.

'Shame on you, boy.' Baraju smiled. 'Stop sniffling. Don't be a sissy.'